THE LAST MAN ON EARTH

By Stephen J. Phillips

Published by
Stephen J. Phillips
Folkestone, Kent
United Kingdom

www.phillips-writer.co.uk
stephen@phillips-writer.co.uk

Copyright ©2018 Stephen Phillips
This edition ©2020 Stephen Phillips
ISBN: 9798679509979

Also from Stephen Phillips:

Science Fiction:
Ozymandias (Book I of the Ozymandias trilogy)
Heraclitus (Book II of the Ozymandias trilogy)
Zarathustra (Book III of the Ozymandias trilogy)

Historical:
The Ice Cream Seller
Raptor

The Pitt Family series (13th Century):
The French Carpenter
The Templar Pitt
The Goldsmith's Apprentice

Acknowledgements

I would like to thank all those who checked the initial drafts
of this book, especially Hilary Tyler and my brother, Nigel
Phillips, both of whom made very useful suggestions, as
well as commenting on the text itself. Any mistakes remain
my own.

Contents

Prologue

I'm standing shivering on the battlements of a castle in the middle of a storm of arrows. Fletched missiles and crossbow bolts whistle past my head and I've nothing with which to fight back. No sword, no battle axe, not even a small knife – just a flimsy shield. Soon, the arrows will stop flying and the hoards beneath me will scale their ladders, surmount the stone crenellations which are my sole defence against these unknown invaders, and slaughter me.

It's so dark, I can't see anything except the glint of metal weapons reflected in the milky moonlight. Weird sounds come from in front of me as well as below. It's as if my enemy has dragons, or massive birds of prey ranged against me and there's nothing I can do to defend myself.

A grappling hook bites into the stonework next to me. It's not only ladders they're using. I have no choice but to turn and flee, scampering along the narrowing walkway which is the only thing between the attackers on one side and a fifty-foot fall to oblivion in the courtyard on the other. Why is it shrinking? Why do I feel as if I am running through a muddy field, rather than along a stone passage? I head for the door leading to a guardroom and access to a tower above. Perhaps I can hide there and escape detection.

Behind me I hear hounds. Not stopping to wonder how they reached the top of the walls, I dive through the door and slam it behind me. I look for something to bar it, but I can't see anything. Am I blinded by my terror, or is it simply too dark? Or is my mind tricking me?

Suddenly, the door opens. It's daylight, but nobody is outside on the verdant green grass stretching out in front of me for miles. There is no path, yet I know if I follow the rising sun, I'll be safe. Behind me, I hear the hounds again. They've somehow followed. I glance round to see if the warriors are with them, but all I can see is the snarling blood-stained teeth of two massive dogs. If there are any handlers with them, I can't see because of the bright light emanating from the room I've just left.

I run onto the narrow stony path which has suddenly unfolded before me, tripping and stumbling in my haste to escape. Somehow, I evade the hounds which seem now to be wading through a stream, apparently losing my scent. I run an impossible distance, hoping nothing can keep pace. My pounding heart seems to have a rhythm of its own, like the beating of distant drums.

Now the sounds are ahead of me. I'm running through a jungle and towards a clearing. In it, tribesmen beat out a tattoo on hollowed wooden logs; a death threat, a warning, or messages of friendship? Doubtless it's the first – a threat that unseen hands will soon drag me down to the depths of a hell I can't comprehend.

Something grabs hold of my legs. It is the liana of a tree which has noiselessly stretched itself across the path and wound round my ankles, dragging me down. As I fall, I don't hit the ground, but rather fall into a deep pit. An animal trap – designed for large animals, I guess from the size. The liana won't let go and I find myself suspended upside-down, dangling above a pointed spike. I'm trapped.

Something tugs at my legs and I feel myself being pulled up out of the hole. To face what? Tribesmen? Viking warriors? Ravening dogs?

Nothing. Nothing at all. Just whiteness. I must be dead.

'Wake up,' says a disembodied voice. 'You must stop reading ancient history last thing at night. You need a hobby.'

Chapter 1 – A message in a bottle

W hy am I writing this? If you can call talking into a recording machine 'writing'. It's not as if anyone will ever see it. There's nobody left, but me. And I'm reaching the stage where I don't know if I want to carry on much longer. It's not loneliness, exactly, but I'm not sure I want to be the last man alive. A dubious distinction bequeathed by parents, who decided to bring just one more life into the world before taking their leave of it. Like everyone else.

I'd better introduce myself. My name is Mark. Not that names are relevant anymore. But in the unlikely event that anyone (or anything) intelligent visits Earth in the future, it's a starting point. There's no way of telling whether this message will ever be viewed. But in case it is, I'll give some context, so whoever (whatever) finds it can understand. I'll move the camera lens around my home and describe what you see. That way pictures and words can form your "primer". If I were cleverer, I might construct some sort of binary message of ones and noughts, enabling an intelligence to break the code of our language. As it is, I'll simply rely on the images and the written word which syncs with my voice, to act as a guide. Good luck.

This is the room in which I live. The walls are white with clear windows cut into them for seeing outside. I'll come to that later. First, let's see how I live. Over there is a table and upright chairs used largely for eating my meals. There are several chairs as a throwback to the days when visitors might come. I sit on a different one each day, to provide a little variety. By variety, I mean not doing the same thing all the time. Here, I'll sit on one of the chairs and then another, so you can see what I mean. I should explain that the machine on which this is being recorded is automated. I think where I want it to point and it does so. Sometimes, I'll be in the picture; others not.

Over there are two more comfortable chairs for me to relax. Not that there's much else for me to do. I don't have to work to provide my food and other necessities, that's done by machines. Once, they were humaniform – looked very much like us – but some found this disconcerting, so we decided they should look like machines, instead.

Perhaps boredom is why I'm creating this record. Rather like the diaries our ancestors used to keep, recording their daily lives, feelings and so on. I've read some of them. They vary from amusing – like one by a man called Tom Jones, or Henry Fielding, I'm not quite sure which – to deeply harrowing, like one by a young woman called Anne Frank.

There are other rooms for sleeping, washing and performing the other functions which so wearied my race. I still do them, of course, but for how much longer can I be bothered?

I've one other thing to show you – a computer terminal. I call it Albert, after Einstein, the father of atomic science. It controls everything in my home, as well as much outside. Albert was once my main source of communication with the world. But for many years, there's been only silence when I've tried to contact anyone. Not very impressive, is it? Just a screen, really. But I was told it can perform trillions of calculations a second. I sometimes wonder whether Albert still communicates with other computers, somewhere. But I've no way of telling. I don't understand it very much.

Before I give you some of our history, I'll show you outside.

The countryside is made up of green grass and leaves, brown tree trunks and branches and regular splashes of colour which are flowers. The flowers are brightly coloured to attract insects and birds for fertilisation.

It wasn't always so pretty, with rolling hills and gentle valleys. Once, it was full of concrete buildings, few of any artistic merit. And roads, to facilitate travel, making ugly grey gashes across what countryside there was. There was a time when millions lived cheek by jowl. Each needing somewhere to live and – once – to work. There were shops and factories, offices and places of entertainment. Of course, this was part of the problem. Too many people and too few natural resources. More of which later.

Looking across the valley to your right, the colours become less distinct. That's because the atmosphere carries particles of dust which blur our view. It used to be much worse; something called pollution made the air thick with dirt and chemicals. But not now. Not for thousands of years. The sparking ribbon of blue at the bottom of the valley is a small river, reflecting the sunlight like a million diamonds. It's teeming with life. Fish live in it and other animals visit to drink its crystal-clear water. We used to catch, cook and eat them all. Humanity was at the top of the food chain for a long time. Almost no animal was safe from us. But now we – I mean I – only eat what can be grown in the fields round the house. Or synthesised by Albert. Perhaps I should have mentioned we can replicate almost anything we want. Anything *I* want.

There are some birds flying in the sky to your left. I don't know what they are called, but there are sometimes so many in a flock, they seem to darken the sun, like thick clouds. You can see light clouds in the distance. They provide the rain which feeds the river. But it never rains here.

I've turned the camera round so you can see the outside of my home. Well, you can see the entrance and windows.

Most of the rooms are built into the hillside, a throwback to some of the problems we experienced a long time ago.

I should provide some context for what's happened on this planet. Earth, we called it; to you it might be Sol III – the third planet from the sun.

Humanity has been around for hundreds of thousands of years in one form or another. You could argue we go back almost thirty million years, to the first great apes, from which we descend. But our true ancestors probably appeared about two and a half million years ago. By other measures, modern man developed physically about 250,000 years ago, with what we understand as 'people' evolving about 120,000 years ago. About that time, Homo Sapiens – it means wise man, which is probably something of a joke – leached out over the planet from its home near the equator, to become ubiquitous. 50,000 years ago, humanity discovered atomic power, initiating the developments which brought us here.

Where is 'here'?

Well, I suppose a situation where we are functionally extinct. There's no evidence of any other living person on this planet. Believe me, I've been trying to make contact for almost a century. We are by no means the first species to die out; nor will we be the last. Some have arguably been more successful than us. By the most generous interpretation, we've survived for less than thirty million years. Dinosaurs lived at least five times as long, more than two thirds of that time as the dominant species. We only managed dominance for the blink of an eyelid, by comparison.

On the other hand, we created much beauty and grandeur – and ugliness and misery – in a relatively short time. And got off this planet, which no other species managed, as far as we know. Not that reaching Mars (the fourth planet) did any good, given what happened. But we did achieve something in our brief time here. No doubt whatever comes after us – probably termites and other insects – will do just as well. Or better. But will they bother to record their achievements? Other species didn't. Perhaps that is why I am recording this …

Time to try once more to contact someone … anyone … who can respond. Albert sends a recorded voice message across a broad spectrum of frequencies, as well as an electronic 'handshake'. He doesn't need me to do it, but I like to be there. Just in case.

If anyone *is* still alive on Earth, they should hear. Not that anyone has, so far.

Chapter 2 – Decline and fall

I've ordered my thoughts since I last recorded. I was beginning to ramble – rather like my more chaotic dreams, but I don't want to talk about those. I'll give you a brief history of humanity since shortly before the Atomic Era, as we call it, began.

I'm 130 years old; the prime of a life which should reach 250 years, or more. In an earlier age, I'd be settling down with a partner to raise a family. Like my own parents did at about this age. Having children has changed very little since the earliest days of humanity. Well, procreation was the same. And despite all humanity's medical progress, giving birth never became any easier for women. Childcare, however, became increasingly remote, as more technology became involved. I wonder if this was one of the issues which altered mankind's self-perception and led to its decline?

I had a conventional childhood up to the age of about thirty, when my parents decided they'd had enough. Not of me – I was a relatively docile child – but of the world. My education was like that of every previous generation for thousands of years. I had no friends, of course. There weren't any others around. I was given a liberal education by Albert's predecessor. It covered history – to which I paid little attention, although I'm more interested now – as well as the visual arts and music, both of which I enjoyed. Science and engineering was something for computers; of no value to people. But I took to philosophy, learning about how people used to think and the impact this had on their lives. Unfortunately, I'd nobody other than the teaching computer to discuss my ideas with. My parents paid little attention to me, being more interested in each other and their own studies. Father was fascinated by ancient religions and mother spent much of her time trying to understand animals and how they lived. An equally arcane subject, I felt. Most of my time was spent learning to play musical instruments. Which they probably thought as strange as I felt their interests to be. We lived virtually separate lives as I grew up. When they suddenly left, I hardly noticed.

In fact, for four or five weeks, I didn't realise they were no longer about. The house is quite large – I've only shown you the rooms I use – so we seldom crossed paths. I heard them together sometimes, at night, but took no interest. I had my computer for all the companionship I needed. Virtual reality is far better than the 'real thing', I believe.

My parents decided to move on and did so without a second thought for me. But why should they consider my interests? I was perfectly capable of looking after myself. Parents haven't taken part in their children's upbringing for more generations than I can imagine.

In the time before humanity discovered how to split the atom, it had spent almost its entire time fighting with itself. In some cases, it was ostensibly about religion. But according to father, on a rare occasion when I challenged him about it, this was obfuscation. Most wars, he argued, were about power, land, energy, hatred or simply the desire to conquer and rule others. Religion, he said, was only ever an excuse. Rulers and religious leaders had exercised their skills in convincing perfectly reasonable people to do morally indefensible things in the name of *their* deity.

A pacific man, father hated the very idea of war. It was so destructive and wasteful. But he admitted that most scientific progress came in times of conflict and this was certainly true of the development of atomic power. The beginning of our era – and of humanity's decline.

After bringing the world to the edge of destruction, people started to use atomic fission for energy, instead of war. It proved highly volatile, and massive accidents lead to thousands being mutilated or killed. And still the threat existed of its use in war. For centuries, there was a thing called 'mutually assured destruction' whereby several blocs possessed the ability to annihilate their enemies – and destroy the entire population of the world. Gradually, the appetite for weapons of mass destruction waned – but fighting continued, on and off.

As the population grew, demand for energy increased in proportion, as did the need for ever greater supplies of food. Mass migrations followed the pattern of those seen in earlier ages, which led to heightened tension between nations. (Nations were groups of people living in roughly the same place.) Potential disaster was averted when scientists harnessed nuclear fusion as a safer form of energy, virtually free and plentiful. This allowed them to control the weather, facilitating greater productivity in growing crops. Lower meat consumption also made it easier for food production more to satisfy demand.

Things started to go wrong when 'employment' became scarce.

In the distant past, people had worked – either for themselves or others – to ensure the basic needs of life: food, shelter and clothing. An ancient philosopher called Maslow even developed this into a 'Hierarchy of needs', just before the atom was first split. He defined physiological needs, safety, a sense of belonging as the basics, followed by the esteem of others and then self-actualisation, as the motivation for everything we do.

Except for the very young, the very old – and the very rich – everyone had to earn a living by creating things, or offering services, which others wanted. The idea of infinite leisure to enjoy the fruits of other people's labour has always been a dream, I imagine. But the practicalities were rather different.

The ability to create everything society might want at little real cost sounds attractive. But it leads to two outcomes.

First, all the wealth becomes concentrated in the hands of a few people, unless society is structured in such a way that everyone has a fair share – which it never is. This leads to conflict, as some believe they are receiving a smaller share than they are entitled to, while others live luxurious lives for little effort. An old philosophy book I read argued 'from each according to his ability, to each according to his needs', which seems eminently sensible, but requires what historians called a directed economy. Whenever this was tried, new sets of rulers arose to impose their own order – and most people remained effectively dispossessed. If there's no need for individual effort, it should be easy to order society to satisfy everyone's requirements. But it never seemed to work that way, especially with a growing population.

The second issue is subtler. 'The devil makes work for idle hands' is an ancient proverb. As people worked less to satisfy their needs, they found time pressing on them. They wanted to do something, but had no structure to follow. Leisure pastimes such as competitive sport grew in importance, until tribalism – the desire to belong to an identifiable group and support it against all others – led to increasing levels of violence. Before long, sporting events became an excuse for pitched battles and the authorities had to clamp down. Leaving a vacuum; which nature is said to abhor.

No commonly accepted reason existed for the wars which took place during the early centuries of the Atomic Era. For some, it was exponential population growth, driven partly by increased leisure making procreation one of the most popular ways of filling time. For others, the improvements in health standards, leading to increasing longevity allowed greater numbers of elderly people to block progress for younger ones in what few careers remained.

Religions also started to lose much of their control over believers, which was a mixed blessing, if I might permit myself a modest pun (I'll explain puns and jokes later). Organised religions were once seen as a way of ordering society and the behaviour of its members. By threatening future damnation, or holding out the promise of eternal bliss, it was possible to regulate the actions of adherents. As the influence of spiritual leaders waned, for a variety of reasons, their ability to prevent people's worst excesses withered like unpicked grapes. (I enjoy making wine.) Conversely, since some opponents argued religious intolerance was responsible for much of the violence of the pre-Atomic and early Atomic Era, its absence might have been considered a benefit.

Whatever the causes, tensions grew between nations and war seemed perennial. Unlike the major conflagrations at the end of the pre-Atomic age, there were few stable alliances. Groups morphed from one alliance to another, to reflect the whims of their leaders and changes in their interests, as predicted by the philosopher George Orwell in his strangely titled thesis, 1984.

After a century of free-for-all fighting, much of it using weapons of mass destruction, the population had shrunk below the levels required to sustain further conflict. The world subsided into a 'dark age', alleviated only by the scientific advances too ingrained to be lost. Humanity ended the fourth century of the Atomic Era vastly reduced, but with the ability to survive. Provided it avoided further conflict.

For hundreds of years, humanity rubbed along. Science produced better ways to co-exist, with the use of robots being investigated. This wasn't the first time, but previous attempts were frustrated by the limits imposed by computing capacity and the energy to power complex machinery for long periods. Fusion solved this problem, as power units could now be made sufficiently small. A generator the size of a pea can power many homes for decades.

Humanoid robots rapidly became unpopular as some people became jealous of their ability to do everything perfectly. This may have caused problems within intimate relationships, according to some salacious ancient reports.

They were, however, ideal for the newly reinvented science of astrophysics. Human-shaped robots could be sent into space for immensely long periods without any concern about their physical – or mental – wellbeing, despite the long timescales involved. They didn't need to be humaniform, but if people were to follow, it made sense to have them create – and live in – environments which would favour mankind.

Reaching Mars was simple, and a colony of humans quickly followed the robots which established a foothold there. The Moon was never seen as a viable option after the disastrous war there shortly into the Atomic Era. Terraforming Mars took a thousand years, largely because it was difficult to increase the planet's atmosphere to a sustainable level, until someone had the idea of sending robotic spaceships to bring back water from the asteroid belt. This gave a lifeless planet the liquid essential to life, and increased its mass so it could sustain a thicker atmosphere.

Not far beyond the asteroid belt is Jupiter. Its many satellites have long intrigued humanity and one, Europa, was known to have a massive ocean beneath a crust of ice. Scientists sent robotic spacecraft to investigate, in the hope of finding life. They did, of course, but nothing with what we recognise as intelligence.

That's what we thought about the dinosaurs – and look how much better than humanity they did.

There was nothing on the outer planets and their moons for humanity. We couldn't easily live there so the search went further afield, right to the edge of the solar system. That took the best part of another century. The journey was much faster than the first voyage of discovery there, which took over 35 years at the start of the Atomic Era. But designing and building a spacecraft capable of reaching 100 times as fast – just 0.5% of the speed of light – took the combined resources of seven universities 50 years.

And of course, reaching the edge of the solar system in four months was never going to get humanity to the nearest star. That's four light years away. The trip there took eight centuries. Two and a half millennia after the first man-made atomic reaction, humanoid robots reached our nearest neighbour. There they found a habitable planet, as (apparently) forecast.

Not that this did much good. During the intervening period, manned space travel had taken a step backwards.

Time to try once more to see if there's anyone out there. I sometimes wonder if it's worth the effort. But if I don't at least try, I might go mad. Albert is not wholly satisfying as a companion.

Chapter 3 – Is anybody there?

That was unexpected. Yesterday, I arranged for Albert to send out the usual greeting messages. I do so at different times each day, partly to vary my routine but also because – should there be anyone (or anything) out there, I wouldn't want my messages to be mistaken for background noise. An irregular pattern of structured signals should indicate intelligence at this end. After all, a regular recorded message might have been created hundreds of years ago and simply repeated by a machine. There's enough stored power for this to happen for thousands of years without human intervention.

What caused my excitement – yes, I find I'm capable of emotion after all – was the apparent existence of a reciprocal carrier-wave. I don't understand the technicalities, but Albert detected a live transmitter on one of the frequencies we use. There could be several explanations, such as an old radio which still has power and might somehow have become activated. Perhaps an animal nudged something which made it go live. It could be an automated system which only operates occasionally. Of course, my transmitting times are erratic, but given how long I've been sending messages, we should have coincided more than once. Albert can't have missed a previous potential interaction. He's programmed not to.

There's another option. Might there be someone out there?

I'm not sure how I feel about the possibility. I've been alone so long. I partly crave companionship and partly dread it. Could I co-exist with someone else? Would I want to? Would anyone else want to live with me? What if we didn't like each other? Of course, these are all academic questions. There's probably nobody there, and even if there is, we needn't meet. Or to spend much time together. I'm excited by the prospect of at least not being alone.

The issue of how I might react to another person's physical presence isn't immediate. Albert can't precisely locate the signal's origin. Nor has there been any message on which we could base assumptions. Or even ask whoever – or whatever, let's not forget that – is at the other end. If anyone.

For all our technological progress over so very long, some skills remain beyond us. Locating the source of a signal from one location might once have been possible, but not now. Albert says we need to hear the same signal from a second position, to 'triangulate' its point of origin.

One positive is that, as soon as he identified a possible second radio signal, Albert went into continuous listening mode. The carrier-wave is active periodically at the other end. Surely, that cannot be a coincidence? Please!

Well, that answers one question. I'm not satisfied to be the last human being after all. If there's someone out there, I want to meet them – or at least have some contact. This calls for action.

The carrier-wave is coming from the south. I live in the northern hemisphere on a large land mass. There are plenty of places on that trajectory which could be populated, but they might be 70 miles or 7,000 miles, for all I know. The signal is very weak, which suggests a great distance, but Albert says travelling 40 miles due east should be sufficient to pinpoint the transmission however far away it is.

Albert could send a drone, but I think I'll go myself. It's been too long since I went anywhere.

Well, I didn't anticipate that. Albert's being obstructive. He says it's too dangerous for me to travel beyond the estate and insists on sending a drone to get the second directional bearing. I don't agree and tell the damned machine he has no right to nanny me. I'm perfectly capable of leaving home for a few days. Provided he gives me all the equipment I'll need.

At last. Albert's relented and agreed to facilitate my trip, provided he can send a couple of drones for my "protection".

I must admit to some trepidation about what I'm doing. I'll carry on recording my observations. Just in case …

It's my first day away from the house in many decades and the sun is disappearing below the hills behind me. I don't recall having seen this from outside my home, before. It's disconcerting; the sudden chill might be natural, or emanate from my nerves. But I'm not in any physical danger. Albert has ensured that by sending the drones. I've shelter and food to keep me going for a month, not six days. I opted not to carry anything; Albert's drones have their uses. But I'm unaccustomed to so much walking and I'm glad I brought a stick to lean on – and for balance when crossing streams or rough terrain. It's centuries since people travelled sufficiently to need roads, or even paths. So, there's no easy way to cover the ground. I suppose I could have taken up Albert's offer to build a vehicle. But I was so cross with his nannying, I insisted on walking. Mistake.

The transport drone has landed by a clump of trees and I'm unpacking what I need for the night. A canvas cover – Albert called it a tent – is easy to put up. Push a button on the casing and it auto-erects. It even drove some stakes into the ground to stop it moving in a strong wind. I'd have thought it was heavy enough already, but what do I know? There's a chair for me to sit on and a small table for eating

THE LAST MAN ON EARTH

at. A lamp hangs on the front of the tent, so I can see what I'm doing, but at least I don't have to cook my meal. The radio detector drone doubles as a valet. I don't need one at home, there are systems to tidy up after me. Here, the drones must do everything.

While they prepare a necessarily basic evening meal, I have time to watch the fading light. Finally disappearing below the horizon, the sun gave way to a gradually darkening night. First a few stars, then hundreds and eventually countless thousands appeared, creating a vast river of light above my head. I'd like to pick out the constellations envisaged by various ancient races, but don't know sufficient about them. Indolence – or shame at my ignorance – prevents me from asking the drones.

After eating, I enter the tent to rest. I'm tired, but not dissatisfied with the unaccustomed exercise. I fell asleep almost immediately.

I wake up frightened, as if from a dream. It's not cold, but I'm shivering. There are noises outside I've never heard before. They must be animals. And large ones by the sound of them. Is this what Albert was worried about?

Sitting up, I pull on my coat and creep to the front of the long, narrow tent. I can still hear movement outside. The moon is casting a massive shadow onto the canvass. If that's an animal, it's one I've never seen – or even heard of. It must be at least three metres tall. Much bigger than me. And wide. Almost as wide as it is tall. The edges are irregular, as if it has been mauled in a fight. God knows what animal out here is large enough to injure this monster.

Reaching carefully through the opening, I switch on the light outside the tent, hoping to scare the beast off. But it doesn't move. Not away – but not towards me either. I wish I'd let Albert fashion some sort of weapon for me. But I told him I didn't need one. Idiot.

There's no alternative. I must look outside. If I make a lot of noise, the monster might flee. After all, it's undoubtedly never seen a human. I may be smaller, but I have intelligence and speed. So here goes.

It wasn't an animal. It was just the shadow of a large bush, the moonlight throwing a gently undulating – and highly intimidating – image against the canvas of the tent. I change my underwear and return to bed.

Morning seems so different from the night. The light is clearer than I've ever noticed, the grass on which I pitched my tent is damp and smells musty. But in a nice way. All my life has been lived indoors. Perhaps I might spend more time in the open. Especially in the mornings. I can hear birds singing to each other – or perhaps to themselves, just for the joy of being alive. And there are no large animals about. Just a few squirrels and other woodland creatures of which I don't know the names.

Clearing the camp, the drones and I set off in the same direction as before, initially heading for the sun, before allowing it to swing round to my right, by the middle of the day, before having it increasingly warming my back.

OK, I'll be honest. The drones kept me heading due east, but I can fantasise about having the navigational skills of a Magellan, can't I?

My route isn't direct; there are obstacles. Hills, valleys and large rock outcrops block the way. But most of these are easily climbed, crossed, or circumvented. And the exercise is invigorating. Muscles I didn't know about are aching, but as each mile passes I feel more alive than for a long time. The detector drone provides occasional comments on topography, or a report from Albert on something inconsequential. I begin to wonder if he needs my company as much as, I suppose, I benefit from his. But that's a little like the way people used to think about domestic pets. Imputing human emotions to them was called anthropomorphising. Dogs didn't really smile; cats never really look superior.

By the end of the second day, I've covered almost 35 miles. According to the detector drone, I'll reach the position Albert indicated to set up the triangulation some time tomorrow morning.

We follow the same routine as last night except, this time, I enjoy the experience of being *alfresco*. That the tent walls are so fragile no longer worries me. I've found a stout stick to serve as a primitive weapon. It'll ward off anything which might come near. And I'm ready for shadows tonight.

Damn. I slept much later than intended. This might not matter, but we need to be in position before the next potential signal comes through. There's still nothing more than the hiss of a carrier wave, but it now occurs at predictable times. The signal starts exactly a day after the previous forty-minute transmission ends. The last transmission was, according to Albert, at noon, yesterday, so we need to be in place by half past twelve, to be ready. If I move quickly, I should be in time. I could send the detector drone on ahead, but I want to be there. Would humans have discovered North America, had they sent their robots out looking? Possibly. But it would have been less of an achievement.

We made it with an hour to spare. The detector drone is hovering ten metres above me, ready to locate the bearing of the signal and I'm listening in on a speaker. Just in case we get more than the usual hiss.

There it is! The carrier wave is right on time. Detector drone has the signal clearly, although it's as weak as ever. The direction is still almost due south, but not quite. Even I know this means it must be a very long way away. Albert can do the calculations – probably already has – but I'm guessing we're looking at the southern hemisphere for a point of origin. Might be closer, but not much.

A thought strikes me. This would place the message as coming from Africa, from whence early humans migrated some 120,000 years ago. Coincidence?

I should feel please at my little adventure. But instead I'm deflated. There was nothing new in the signal and there's still the journey back. I could carry on walking eastwards for a few days, but there's no 'excitement' waiting for me out there. Might just as well return to the old routine, even though I'm already wondering whether that's what I want anymore. Yet, travelling through uninhabited lands – even a very short way – has been exhilarating. Perhaps I should do this again. I could travel further and see completely new things. Even meet new monsters! I laugh at myself for having been frightened by a bush.

As I set off for home, Albert is surprisingly quiet. He sends few messages and I wonder if he somehow resents my having had this adventure. But that's ridiculous. Nevertheless, I'm disconcerted to find his silence worries me.

I reach home at the end of the second day after taking the reading. Five days in total; the longest I've been away for fifty years or more.

Slumping down in my chair, I listen to what Albert says with the half-attention of a tired man trying to ignore being told what his children have been doing all day. Eventually, it impinges on my mind that he wants something. Thinking back, I recall him mentioning an anomaly. I wonder what it was all about, so ask him to repeat it. He does so with audio effects.

I find it difficult to hear what I'm supposed to be listening to. The carrier wave is there as usual, but just as it ends, there is a definite sound which differs from what went before. To my fanciful mind, it's a voice. It might even be saying 'again' as if at the end of a sentence. But why would we suddenly receive a single word over the ether? Albert says it might be simply the radio wave bouncing off the ionosphere in a propitious way so that we hear something. But this seems unlikely, since it should have happened before.

Chapter 4 – Making contact

There's something else. Albert reports the signal as being from farther away than possible. The circumference of the Earth is about 24,000 miles, so the signal should be coming from no more than 7-8,000 miles. The triangulation indicates it is coming from nearer a quarter of a million miles. Roughly the distance of the moon's orbit. This could be an error in the drone's data, but Albert thinks it unlikely. I agree he can send it out alone – I can't face another walk quite so soon – over a much greater distance and take another reading. It can do it in a single day. So tomorrow, a little after lunchtime, we should have confirmation.

The wait is almost unbearable. The drone has flown a hundred miles to the west this time and should receive the signal soon. We're listening in too, of course. It's past time for my meal, but I can't eat anything; I'm too excited. Might we hear another human voice? Might we be able to tell where it's coming from?

At just before twenty past one, we hear the carrier wave. Albert issues the usual electronic 'handshake' for any listening machines, as well as the voice message we always use.

This time, there is no mistaking the presence of a voice at the other end. It's almost impossible to pick up more than a word or two and the nature of the speaker is unidentifiable. But it is certainly speaking English and seems to understand we are transmitting too.

There really is someone alive, other than me. I never believed it possible. My cautious mind had insisted this was probably an ancient recording we'd intercepted. But there's certainly interaction of sorts. No automated transmission could emulate that.

As I absorb this information, Albert announces his findings. He was wrong, it wasn't a quarter of a million miles. It was 25 million miles. A tenth of the way to Mars. A dead planet for millennia.

This can't be human, but something else with which we are in embryonic conversation. Is this 'first contact' with another species? If so, how have they learned our language? But Albert has been transmitting for so long our messages must have reached many light years into space by now. They might have given an intelligent race an introduction to our way of communicating. Have I brought some unimaginable creatures down on myself? If so, I've only myself to blame for whatever happens. Finding a virtually uninhabited planet, my visitors may decide to colonise Earth. And kill me. Or keep me as a pet.

No, that doesn't work. Even if my message had reached 50 light years away, even the most advanced intelligence couldn't have reached something like the speed of light to arrive so quickly.

On the other hand, humanity has been sending signals into space for more than 50,000 years. A thousand times longer for something to identify the source of the signals and mount a safari to investigate. Travelling at 1% of the speed of light – even more – is far from impossible.

Either way, something is coming. I wait with mixed emotions for tomorrow's radio exchange.

OK, that was overly optimistic. It's a week before our visitors are close enough for us to discern anything intelligible. We know they're heading here, because Albert is tracking their trajectory. He says they are coming from something like the position Mars must have been in the best part of a year ago. This doesn't prove anything, but it's suggestive. We continue listening and Albert has developed an algorithm to alert us when language becomes clearer, should we miss it.

Early one morning, we finally hear something we can understand.

'Hello, can you hear me now?' It's a female voice. 'I've boosted my signal and am sending data which might help you do the same.' Albert reports having received the package and quickly works out how to modify it for our use. She must be bright to have thought of something even my computer couldn't, to improve communications. But perhaps he hadn't bothered.

By the end of the day, I can respond. Now contact is established, we're no longer following the old 24.67-hour time pattern

'Hello, this is Mark Adams, speaking from Earth. What's your name and how many of you are there?'

A deafening silence stretched through three long minutes. Were they deciding how to respond? To tell the truth, or obfuscate in the hope of gaining an advantage later?

Finally, the speaker bursts into life again.

'Sorry for the delay, Mark. As you must have realised there's one-and-a-half-minute time delay on our messages, due to the distance. I'm Evelyn Starr. Can you transmit a picture?'

That's promising. If she was asking that, she must be prepared to reciprocate, which reduced the risk of obfuscation. I respond quickly to show good faith.

'Yes, Evelyn. It'll take a little time as we are not geared up for this, but we'll be able to send and receive images by tomorrow. That OK?' I want time to think about whether this is a good idea, but can't see a reason not to.

Again, a wait. Imperceptibly shorter, as the spacecraft closed at 35,000 miles an hour.

'That's good, Mark. I look forward to seeing you then. 'Bye.' This time the connection broke off from the other end. Saving power?

While Albert works on linking my recording device to the transmitter, so Evelyn and I can see each other, I allow myself to contemplate what this all meant. She's given no information about where she comes from, or her purpose in making what must be a monumental journey. The name and colloquial expression – what little she spoke – suggested a shared heritage. Only two possibilities occurred to me. Three, I suppose, although the last seems impossible. Either she was somehow a survivor from our colony on Mars – which we had thought extinct for the best part of 45,000 years – or she was from another part of Earth and had found the means to get off-planet and travel a very long way. The third option was that she was part of the mission to Alpha Centauri from the same period of our history. But records suggested only robots were sent. Humaniform ones.

I like seeing Evelyn's picture. She looks tall, although there's no real point of reference, and has what I think of as a kind face. Her features are remarkably symmetrical, which makes me wonder if there isn't some artifice involved. I've viewed many pictures from the past and, considering what people apparently found attractive, she seems to fit the bill. Judging by her reaction, she is not completely indifferent to my picture, but the time lag makes it difficult to tell whether her smile is due to relief at receiving the image, or its content.

What I notice most about her face is the obvious tiredness – or is it strain – which seems to furrow her brow when she isn't smiling. Something seems to be wrong.

'Are you travelling alone?' I ask. There's no evidence of others around her and she doesn't seem to have to refer to anyone before speaking. Of course, she might be the captain, alone on her bridge. But she looks very young for that. I put her at no more than 80 years old, her physique showing nothing but agility and freshness.

'I'll tell you more about myself when I land, Mark,' she replies, enigmatically. 'Tell me about where you live. I've been on this spaceship for almost a year and imagine your surroundings are more convivial than mine. I dream about the greens and blues of your planet.' Strange expression that. But I suppose a Martian (if that's what Evelyn is) would no longer see Earth as "home". Not after almost fifty millennia. On the other hand, this is precisely how an alien might express itself. Nevertheless, I share some of the recordings I made earlier, as well as some images from my recent expedition.

While she's looking at the pictures, I'm watching her reaction closely. I see wonder and delight in her eyes – or is that simply the reflection of the screen she's watching? Unless she is a consummate actor, I believe she is genuinely pleased with what she sees. Either Evelyn shares my aesthetic tastes, or she's calculating the value of the planet to her species. Damn, I'm so suspicious. Pull yourself together man.

She seems to expect me to say something. The images stopped moving some time ago, but she is silent, moisture appearing to be running down her face. I've never seen that before.

'Are you alright?' I ask. 'Is anything troubling you?'

After a moment, she forces a smile – even I can tell it isn't natural. 'Yes, I'm fine. Thank you. I've just never seen anything so beautiful.'

Chapter 5 – Changing Earth

While we're waiting to discover more about our mysterious visitor, you might have been wondering why humanity isn't still living on Mars, even if it's extinct here?

It's complicated, but I'll tell you what I know – or think I know – about their history. We'd been there for more than a thousand years before reaching Alpha Centauri. That's more than the longest-surviving continuous empire this planet ever saw. During that time, the so-called red planet experienced many forms of government; most benign, some less so. The existence of advanced technology facilitated the relatively peaceful co-operation of increasing numbers of people. The problem was the way immigrants flocked to the newly terraformed planet. Space travel over what is astronomically a short distance had become inexpensive and easy, so hundreds of thousands made the trip, each year. Most were seeking a challenge to replace what had become an anodyne existence on Earth.

Population growth on Earth tailed off, as the more adventurous left for Mars. Those remaining became indolent, lacking purpose.

Mars could absorb large numbers of settlers. But over the years, tensions developed between those already there and the 'incomers'. Many Martians, as they called themselves, resented new migrants who had contributed nothing towards making the planet hospitable and wanted to reserve some of the best locations and resources for themselves. I suppose this was no different from what has happened on Earth many times, but it paints a sorry picture of humanity. When there's enough space to go around, and plenty of challenges, people seldom resent others coming to join them. As space and resources dwindle, tensions build. And eventually explode. It's not as if immigrants somehow fail to contribute to society; history tells us they always do. But prejudice is a powerful emotion.

Envy, greed, or both raised their heads and before long internecine conflict broke out. Because the earliest settlers had built underground, they were better protected than the newer colonists, who had been able to build homes – and cities – above. The destructive technology available to both sides resulted in the rapid obliteration of many who'd more recently moved there. Soon only a handful of descendants from the earliest families remained in any numbers – and almost no 'incomers'. The survivors had an ingrained mistrust of Earth people.

Gradually, those remaining on Earth heard less and less from Mars. Emigration from the home planet had ceased as soon as the Martian-Immigrant wars started. Naturally. Earth lost interest and by the time robots had reached Alpha Centauri, there may have been nobody left on Mars, as far as those on Earth knew. Or cared.

✻

I'm sorry, I had to break off. I find the thought of an entire civilisation – millions of people – dying out upsetting. I suppose I should feel like that about us on Earth. But somehow, it's not the same.

The thought of taking 800 years to travel to Alpha Centauri seeking a new home appealed to nobody. Well, except a few scientists who were willing to travel in suspended animation with no guarantee of being resuscitated at the end of it. They never went, because nobody would pay for the special equipment needed to survive the trip.

As longevity grew, the population declined. There seemed little imperative to reproduce. Humanity seemed to have lost its ability – or desire – to strive. Perhaps any interest in life itself. New forms of quasi-religion developed.

The most important of these drew on a variety of sources, including the Judaeo-Christian-Islamic tradition, Hinduism and Buddhism. Initially, it strove for a combination of Nirvana (a state in which the mind transcends all suffering and attains peace) and some sort of paradise to be enjoyed after death. The afterlife became increasingly important, compared with the world. You might live for 250-300 years, but would be dead for a lot longer. It was therefore more important to focus on the longer term. People started to neglect themselves in favour of a form of asceticism which saw the mind as more important than the body. This chimed with the beliefs of an ancient (pre-Atomic) cult I read about, the Cathars. These thinkers held the world was the creation not of their God, but of his antithesis, the Devil. As such, they eschewed all aspects of the material existence and looked forward to being released from it through death.

Our new savants modified this, believing they could travel through space and time. For all I know they were right. But an unexpected development apparently put their thinking into context.

One of the movement's leading philosophers claimed an experience which suggested the cult was both right and wrong.

Right, in that there was an alternative to corporeal existence; but wrong, that it was a matter of belief, *per se*. He had 'discovered' a way of detaching the mind from the body, without the need to sustain a physical presence on Earth. It appeared there were no limits to the time a mind could exist. Scientists had long known we use only a small part of our brains and that there was unexplored potential within them. It was always thought, however, that the physical brain was necessary for the mind to function.

The 'breakthrough' – the veracity of which many initially doubted – was that the brain was the seat of the mind, but that it could operate independently. Some critics argued simple belief, without the need for empirical evidence, was the origin of all religions and couldn't be relied on. Others, claimed the heightened state of mind was drug induced. If they were correct, a body was still necessary.

The main issue was one of faith. Those who voluntarily gave up their lives to become body-less minds couldn't communicate with the physical world and its inhabitants. There was copious circumstantial evidence for the truth of the belief. People training to make the transition reported on their experiences of meeting friends who had 'passed over' already. What made it more plausible was that these trainees frequently reported meetings with each other, in another realm, which empirical test suggested could not be the result of collusion. But even so, stories of meeting the dead – there's no other word for it – could simply have been wishful thinking.

Whatever the truth of the matter – and the belief continued until my lifetime – it became universally accepted. What initially started as a way of people continuing their existence at the end of natural life, gradually became a life-choice much earlier.

My own parents 'passed over' when I was thirty. I'd like to say I feel their presence – and that of thirty thousand years' worth of humanity. But I can't. I refused to undergo the training and now I'm the last man left on Earth, as far as I can tell.

I've tried to contact others, I really have. But nobody has responded for decades. There are just the machines and me.

So here I am. Middle-aged and alone. I suppose I could undertake the training and join everyone else. But I simply don't believe in this new state of being.

I see no alternative to living out my natural life alone. Not one which appeals to me, anyway.

Sorry, I was getting ahead of myself. It wasn't just weakness within humanity which led to its decline. Long before the start of the Atomic Era, we started pumping noxious gasses into the atmosphere of our fragile world. For ages, some leaders refused to believe this was damaging the climate. The reason appears to have been the short-termism inherent in the political systems of the time. Governments were elected for as few as four or five years and therefore needed to get re-elected on a regular basis. Politicians put short-term imperatives ahead of long-term considerations. Protecting the climate is expensive and takes generations to show any benefit. Successive governments therefore deferred taking essential action which might have avoided catastrophe.

At about the same time as we started to be able to generate clean and almost free energy, slowing climate change, a new and virulent disease struck humanity. This plague was a direct result of scientists spending too little time looking for new ways of combatting what were called superbugs. Antibiotics had long been used to counter the effects of bacterial infections, but the bacteria adapt by natural selection – as outlined by a pre-Atomic thinker, Charles Darwin – to resist them. Unfortunately for humanity, insufficient resources were put into researching new ways to fight bacteria and as they became resistant to the most advanced antibiotics, a new disease suddenly became endemic in parts of the world. Without natural resistance, vast swathes of humanity died before an antidote could be created. Naturally, it went first to the richest nations, but this had the effect of reducing the world population dramatically, for centuries.

The only positive result was a lowering of demand for those things which contributed most to air pollution. Over the course of several millennia, the climate returned to what was understood to be the pattern in the thousand years before Atomic Era. There were, of course extreme events, massive storms, floods and droughts, but these tended to be far less frequent than during the worst period of history. (Recorded history only extends about five thousand years before the Atomic Era, but geological evidence gives an indication of conditions in earlier times.)

During the last forty millennia, the planet had passed through many cycles affecting climate, even a long-overdue change in magnetic polarity, some decades into the current age. Many volcanoes remain active and new islands form occasionally. But the planet is generally more stable than ever before. I can't help wondering whether this calming of a previously violent world was not a contributory factor to a sense amongst humanity that it was time to 'move on'. As 'temporal' challenges reduced, did we become more 'spiritual', feeling it was no longer worth striving to survive?

Perhaps it would have been better had we pursued space travel more vigorously, without hiding behind robots. We'll never know.

Today, the climate, at least here, is pleasant. Adequate sunshine and rain encourage the growth of flora – and my grapevines – while I can enjoy a gentle modulation of the seasons. Animal life is also now more diverse than at any time since humanity's actions resulted in species becoming extinct at the rate of more than a hundred a day. Nature has a way of creating new life despite our best endeavours.

Looking through my window, I see a bewildering array of animal life. It cohabits peacefully, except when hunger rouses one or other to action. Unlike humanity, animals seldom kill for any reason other than to eat.

Chapter 6 – Landing

I'm not surprised Evelyn was emotional at seeing pictures of Earth, after all. The terraforming of Mars could never have reached the stage where vistas like those I've shown her developed. I'd never really thought about it, but Earth took billions of years to become what it is. How could I have expected such loveliness to have been achieved in fewer than 50 millennia?

It's time for me to do some research. Seeing her eyes filling with tears made me think back to my youth. Rarely, strong emotion made my eyes water; like when a favourite pet died, or a computer programme didn't work. But I'd never seen it happen to anyone else, so somehow never wondered what it looked like. Now I'm interested to see whether such emotions have ever been recorded in art.

I'm strangely moved. Tears have been represented in art, both photographic and painted images, many times. At first, it can be distressing to wonder what caused the reaction. Pain? Loss? Frustration? But looking at the faces it's clear that joy and love can also cause crying. Thinking back to Evelyn, yesterday, I try to imagine what it might have been in her case. Yet while her picture is clear enough, it didn't open a window into her soul. I can't read her emotions. Perhaps when we meet, it'll be different.

It's time for our daily call. I know I'm not going to find out very much about her, and her people, now. But there are preparations to be made.

'When will you be landing? I must ensure somewhere suitable is ready.'

Evelyn says she will be entering orbit in six days' time and that the craft is capable of landing on any firm flat surface about 150 metres square. Does this give me an indication of the size of the vessel, I wonder? If it needs so much room to land vertically, the craft must be massive. Only something smaller could land horizontally on such a short runway.

'There's a suitable spot not far from here. I'll make sure there is a landing beacon for you. Will you require anything else to help you?' The gap before her reply is getting perceptibly shorter.

'No, thank you Mark. Provided its firm, I can set down gently and my landing gear will accommodate any irregularities.' So, it's a vertical landing, I assume.

'How many of you are there?' I ask, thinking a large ship might accommodate more people than I'm comfortable with. Perhaps I should have selected somewhere further off.

'Don't worry.' She seems to divine my nervousness. 'I'm alone.' Which is more than she would say before. What's changed? 'I'd really appreciate some fresh food when I land. I've been eating space rations for as long as I can remember.

'I'll see what I can do about something special. I don't normally eat meat, but would you like something like that. I'm sure I can find something suitable and get my computer to show me how to prepare it.' She smiles, but shakes her head. She says she only eats vegetables and fruit. Anything I prepare will be fine. We spend almost an hour talking trivia, before I realise how much time has passed and she signs-off, rather abruptly.

Is it possible Evelyn is being held captive and only allowed to talk for a short while – or can only do so while her guards' attention is elsewhere? If so, the statement she's alone is untrue, and I'll need to be alert. Just to be safe. I ask Albert to prepare some weapons of various types and sizes. I'll conceal them around the place, as well as carrying a concealed side arm. At least until I'm confident Evelyn is alone and safe. Do I mean safe from harm, or safe from harming me, I wonder?

The next six days pass more quickly than expected, as I'm busy preparing for Evelyn's arrival. We spend almost an hour every day talking, but still I know little about her or the reason for her journey. I've learned she's been in transit for almost a year and I somehow believe her when she claims to be alone. At least, that she has no companions in whom she can confide. Captors might be another story. Yet this, too, raises questions. Has some faction or other emerged on Mars to vie with others for supremacy? If so, why come to Earth? We have no population left – other than me – and most natural resources were exhausted millennia ago.

But now the day of landing has arrived. Evelyn's craft entered Earth orbit this morning and she will be making the descent to my homemade landing ground, only yards from the house, soon.

A deafening 'boom' cracks the sky open as a tiny object appears high in the air and I fear her ship has exploded. I can't say how bereft I suddenly feel – until I realise I can still see it. I later learn this was the noise of the craft piercing its own soundwave due to its speed. Even I can see it's travelling very fast and I wonder how it can slow sufficiently to land. It goes into a pattern of spiralling turns and loops, each one ending nearer the ground, losing speed with every manoeuvre. It must use some sort of gliding landing, I assume, before realising it's now moving too slowly for that. Powerful engines glow faintly below the body of the craft, which I can see clearly for the first time. They are holding the ship almost stationary as its pilot lines up for a gentle descent onto the field.

The roughly cylindrical vessel is about 100 metres long, I guess, and perhaps a third of that in cross section, tapered at the front and cut off abruptly at the back, as if the builders ran out of ideas. Stubby wings, no more than half the breadth of the craft on either side, appear to give it stability in the atmosphere. I've been reading up on what used to be called aircraft, to see how Evelyn might land. Wings are useless in space, but I wonder if they fulfil any other function.

As it touches down, I feel the mighty draught of its motors as they counter gravity to provide a soft landing, before cutting off.

'Stand back.' Evelyn's metallicized voice breaks the ensuing silence, halting my dash forwards almost before it starts. 'The engines are very hot, and the surface of the craft might be radioactive. Stay there until I can do some checks.' It seems reasonable, so I suspend my impatience to meet the first guest ever to visit. I don't waste my time, however. Walking round the perimeter of the landing field, I look at the strange vessel. The sides are smooth as a mountain washed pebble, and roughly the same colour. As I look more closely, I can see the surface is pitted with small, regularly shaped holes all over. I later discover these are directional thrusters. The main engines nestle between the main body of the craft and its wings. At the back is a completely flat surface, angled so the top overhangs the bottom by several meters. As I walk past, this slowly starts to move, hinged from the base, and the inside of the craft is revealed. A massive empty area – storage space? – surrounds a walkway along the centre of the bottom of the ship, running towards me. Beyond are bulkheads behind which could be just about anything, but, given the height of the doorway leading to the walkway, might be distributed over eight decks. If each level is eighty metres long, that's sufficient space for a significant number of passengers to travel in reasonable comfort. Is Evelyn truly alone?

A slender, elegant woman walks purposefully down the steps I can now see in the middle of the ramp which was previously the back bulkhead of the craft. She's about my height, and more intimidating than when I'd seen her on the screen. In fact, I even wondered momentarily if it might not be her.

She stumbles on reaching the ground and, forgetting my suspicion, I rush forward to help.

'Sorry,' she says, her voice softer than over the radio. 'I'm not accustomed to such strong gravity. On Mars, it's less than half this. I've been increasing the artificial gravity on the ship during the trip, but clearly not enough. Can you help me inside, please?'

I'm surprised how heavy she is. Her bones should be less dense than mine and there's no fat on her. But I suspect she is putting most of her weight on me, suggesting she had miscalculated the difference in gravity quite severely. Or simply failed to make sufficient adjustment. Or is she distracting me, so I don't notice anything else? Well, I'm ahead of her there. I've instructed Albert to monitor the situation carefully, watching for unexpected movement.

I take Evelyn to the quarters I've prepared for her. It's my mother's old bedroom, but I feel no attachment to it. Why should I? I seldom went there when she and father were alive. I imagine Evelyn will appreciate privacy after so long without company – she cannot know what sort of man I am; what I might do to an unprotected woman. If that's what she is.

The room is barely furnished, little more than a bed, table and chairs, on one of which I place her. But it seems to please her. Especially as the bed is only large enough for one. Perhaps she has been worried for her safety. Yet as I turn to leave, she takes my hand as if to prevent my departure.

'Don't go yet. I'm not sick or tired, just rather weak in this gravity. Stay and talk while I gather my strength. Please?'

'Give me a moment.' I reply. 'I want Albert to make something to help you get about. I'll be back shortly.' I truth, I'm overwhelmed by the physical presence of another person and need to escape, even if only for a short while. My chest has tightened, and I feel dizzy – I haven't felt this way since I accidentally locked myself in a cupboard when I was six years old and screamed for hours before my parents noticed I was trapped.

After ten minutes, I've calmed down. Albert has his instructions and has confirmed nobody (or nothing) has left the spacecraft, and there's no evidence of life on board. So at least Evelyn and I are truly alone. I return to her room, to find her sitting in the same position as I left her. I give her a drink from the tray I'm carrying and take one myself.

Chapter 7 – Acclimatisation

Some hours later, Albert alerts me that the device to help Evelyn move about more easily is ready. It's an exoskeleton which will help carry her weight without reducing her range of mobility. It's manufactured from very light material which will be virtually invisible under her clothes. The artificial muscles are far slimmer than those on the human body.

'We've programmed the system so that it provides slightly less support each day,' I tell her. 'That way, you'll increasingly rely on your own body until you don't need the device.' I don't add there is a safety cut off, by means of which I can order Albert to immobilise her. I'm not sure I can trust her completely, so "better safe than sorry".

'How's it powered Mark? Mars used fusion technology, like you, but nothing so small it could be concealed in this device.'

'There's no battery,' I tell her, 'it's powered by microwaves distributed throughout the house. You'll be able to move around inside, and outside for a radius of at least half a mile. You'll never be unable to reach your ship.'

She seems relieved and I realise she probably mistrusts me as much as I doubt her. Yet she had come all this way to find me. I'm confused.

Hoping talking will give me an insight into her motives, I ask her to tell me about herself.

'Whatever you think you know about the history of Mars is probably wrong,' she says, as we sit down in the living room after a light meal. She's unaccustomed to my food and takes a pill to settle her digestion. 'That's not your fault, we deliberately concealed much of our development, to retain our hard-won independence.'

Evelyn's story

Mars (she reminds me) was initially settled about a hundred and fifty years into Earth's Atomic Era, 2093AD in the old calendar. By the end of the following century, thousands of people had moved to the 'Red Planet'. But hostility between factions on Earth had simultaneously resulted in open warfare breaking out here, and the people of Mars kept themselves apart from the hostilities while beginning the long process of terraforming their world. The aim wasn't to create a second Earth, but simply to make the planet more hospitable. Increasing the oxygen levels was a key element and this was achieved by slowly introducing plants in the valleys, where there was at least some air, before moving gradually to higher altitudes. Later they started importing water from the asteroid belt, which increased slowly increased the planet's mass and allowed more oxygen to be retained.

When Earth's wars petered out some quarter of a millennium later, emigration to Mars restarted and, over the course of the next thousand years, terraforming was largely completed. Tensions developed between the older inhabitants and the 'latecomers', resulting in open hostility. (This much I'd known.)

The leadership realised Mars needed to stand alone from the mother planet and decided to create the impression of a terminal decline within the population. Its aim was to discourage further immigration and in this regard, it succeeded. Earth scientists spent centuries reaching into deeper space, largely forgetting its sister planet and eschewing personal travel into space, in favour of sending robots to found new worlds. There was undoubtedly an intention to follow at some stage, but such plans were seldom more than pipe-dreams.

Authorities on Mars continued to monitor developments on Earth, but were careful to give nothing away of their own activities – other than an ongoing impression of social and economic decay.

Over time, they realised Earth was effectively finished. Widespread sickness, brought about by the hubris – or negligence – of scientists who felt capable of manipulating any organism, killed much of the population of Earth. Mars went completely silent, watching while the old world's population took its first slow steps towards a self-destructive cult of decorporealization.

With the home world in decline, Mars could take stock of its position. Unlike (and unknown to) Earth, society there had managed to settle its differences and stabilise its population. Money was outlawed and a truly equitable state of being was created whereby the availability of limitless power and resources enables society to become productive in new ways. People focussed not on the creation of wealth, but pursuing personal fulfilment through art, literature, music, artisan work and pure scientific research.

Humanity had finally reached a state of peace with itself.

For generations things went well for the people of Mars. They enjoyed the fruits of internal peace, and the absence of external threat. Perhaps they relaxed too much. Whatever the cause, it was many centuries before scientists started to notice anomalies in the climate they'd created. Storms increased in severity, daytime temperatures soared towards unseen levels. Nights became unbearably cold. Had it not been for the inherited propensity for living underground, there might have been a catastrophe before anyone was aware of the situation.

Imperceptibly, the atmosphere started to thin as it leached out into space, just as it had done millions of years before humanity had developed past its most primeval level.

Mars – named after an ancient Earth god of war – was fighting back against its enforced 'civilisation'. Ultimately, nature was reasserting itself against humanity's conceit in thinking it could impose its will on a hostile environment. Perhaps, had the people of Mars possessed adequate skills, they might have been able to stem the tide of an irresistible decline towards chaos. But maybe entropy is too great a force of nature to be combatted.

Whatever the case, scientists gradually recognised they had little choice but to abandon their home and seek pastures new.

Earth was an option. Its population was already beginning to abandon its fundamental humanity. The leadership of Mars was aware of the trend towards seeking a less corporeal existence, so there might soon be room for a reverse migration. Mature consideration suggested this was unlikely to be a viable option. It would inevitably involve conflict, for which nobody on Mars had any appetite.

There were only three realistic choices.

One would be to consider expanding out into the universe, as the people of Earth had attempted millennia earlier. And failed. It would be an even greater challenge than returning to Earth, although without the risk of war. The second was to look for an alternative home less remotely. The final choice might be to allow the settlement to die out naturally.

There was time before a decision became essential. Scientists determined the climate wouldn't deteriorate beyond the level at which life was sustainable for thousands of years. But choices must be made within two generations, if adequate plans were to be implemented to save the entire population.

It didn't really take that long to decide what should be attempted. Planning and implementation, however, took the entire remaining time available. And then some. For the last groups to depart, living conditions were like those met by the earliest settlers. Mars had won.

Over the space of a hundred and fifty centuries, five thousand space stations were built, each capable of sustaining thousands of souls. Initially, each was piloted by carefully selected crews who would be naturally self-regenerating over tens of generations while the passengers slept in suspended animation. Each craft was to be sent in a different direction with the aim of giving humanity the greatest chance of surviving the journey. Later, as speeds increased towards a tenth of the speed of light, crews and their passengers could live more normal lives aboard even larger craft, which became practical lifeboats. Entire colonies could survive in space, while actively seeking new homes together.

One development which helped, was the ability to communicate directly between Mars and the various craft, using black-hole technology. Each craft was powered by a fusion plant using a singularity to sustain its integrity and, by 'firing' a digitised message into the singularity, it was possible to send a message to any other known point in space, virtually instantaneously. The speed of light was no longer a limiting factor, at least as far as messages were concerned. As each crew made scientific discoveries, these could be reported to – and verified by – hundreds of scientists in different places. The speed at which knowledge developed became faster than at any time in human history. Equally importantly, each threat encountered by individual spacecraft could be communicated to the others, who could thereby minimise the potential impact on themselves.

Gradually, missions landed on suitable hospitable planets and began the process of settlement. Only those planets which were naturally hospitable to humanity were selected. Terraforming would never again be attempted.

Not once, were any signs of intelligent life identified. Unsurprising, given the vast size of the galaxy and its immense age. Mankind couldn't be the only intelligence to develop in the universe. But the chance of two existing at the same time amongst 200 billion stars over 13 billion years was statistically insignificant. At least, you'd think so.

Chapter 8 – Learning more

E velyn was clearly exhausted by a narration which had lasted several hours. She needed to rest. Then she must undertake some physical activities to strengthen her muscle, I reminded her.

I now understood more about the history of Mars than anyone on Earth had for millennia. As I was unique in every way, this was no distinction. Yet something troubled me. Instead of recording my thoughts, I challenged her directly.

'Why didn't anyone contact Earth, once things started to change?' I asked as she rose from her daybed and moved to the treadmill Albert had constructed.

'I honestly don't know, Mark. I imagine it was a wish to remain separate from you. But it's only a guess. There could have been any number of reasons. Perhaps we were embarrassed by our failure.'

It wasn't the only thing niggling away at the back of my mind. Why had Evelyn decided to come and visit me now? And why alone. Who was behind her trip? I asked.

'OK, it's time to bring you up to date,' she replied.

Evelyn's story (continued)

The massive space station on which Evelyn lived was travelling in the general direction of Alpha Centauri. It had been doing so for more than a thousand years before they identified structured signals which didn't fit the pattern of their communication with other groups. Some of the emigres from Mars were still, like Evelyn's, in transit. Others had decided to remain in permanent 'habitats' in space, while more had settled on suitably hospitable planets. By now more than a thousand colonies had been founded, and it seemed certain that humanity had reached the stage where its ongoing survival was guaranteed. No planetary, even solar system wide, disaster could now extinguish the species. So, unless some inherent genetic anomaly was destined to wipe it out, homo sapiens had achieved something no other known species had before. Racial immortality.

These new transmissions – although they didn't seem to be targeted towards any specific audience – were therefore of interest, but not immediate concern. It could be a hitherto unknown outpost, perhaps a group which had broken away and was only now feeling its way back into the wider community. Yet some scientists on Evelyn's space station had been sufficiently interested to investigate.

The weak signals appeared to be coming from directly ahead. If so, it meant there was already a settlement on their chosen destination. What to do was a topic of discussion. They could change course to avoid entering another colony's province, in case they were unwilling to share their space. Alternatively, they might establish direct contact, to see if their arrival – in many hundreds of years – might be welcome.

Their tentative message was greeted with total silence. Even the original transmissions ceased. In the absence of any discouragement, the captain decided to continue towards Alpha Centauri.

Eventually, short messages started to come from the same source, but this time clearly intended for the space station. The questions asked indicated a complete lack of knowledge of recent history. On Earth, on Mars and its ongoing diaspora. Scientists quickly became concerned. No settlers from Mars could be so ignorant. Had they made first contact with a completely alien species? If so, this was ground shattering – and exciting.

Messages quickly went out to all known Mars ships and settlements. We are not alone.

But how did the aliens know their language, someone finally asked? Scientists assumed this was simply the result of analysis of previous transmissions, but the captain – and ancestor of Evelyn's – was unconvinced. The first time they'd sent a message towards Alpha Centauri, there'd been no response. So, it was now a surprise to hear anything at all. And analysis of the initial communications they'd intercepted suggested these were completely domestic, rather than a deliberate attempt to establish off-world contact. The aliens were apparently previously unaware of their existence, so couldn't have learned their language from previous broadcasts. Either they were incredibly quick learners, or there was something else.

Centuries passed, during which generations of scientists and crew mulled over the possibilities without coming to any conclusions, before anything happened.

Evelyn's mother, herself now captain of the space station, was awoken by an unaccustomed warning claxon. It was an incredibly long time since the proximity alarm had sounded. Once, it had been used to alert navigators to the existence of an obstruction in their path, giving time for it to be safely circumvented. More recently, its use had become redundant, as more sophisticated long-range sensors enabled the crew to anticipate anything large enough to harm the ship well in advance and make gentle corrections. This alarm must relate to some new and unexpected threat.

'Report.' The captain was sufficiently experienced to know she mustn't show concern, but also that this was likely to be significant.

'Captain,' came the voice of her first officer, who was currently on duty, 'it seems to be an interstellar object of little mass, but travelling at impossibly high speed. And it's heading directly towards us.'

Distances were difficult to understand, so the captain asked the more logical question.

'Time to impact, number one?'

'Less than 24 hours,' came the amazed reply. That it could strike them in so short a time meant it must be travelling incredibly fast not to have been noticed earlier. 'I've already initiated evasive manoeuvres, Giselle.' Once rank had been established in an exchange, greater familiarity was customary.

'Thanks, Frank. I'll be with you in half an hour.'

Pausing only long enough to dress and – on an impulse – waken her daughter, a lieutenant commander likely to succeed her one day, Giselle Starr raced to the bridge. Frank's furrowed brow showed all was not well. Evelyn, close in her mother's wake looked at his handsome features and wondered if she would ever get to sleep with him. Probably not, she felt. Mother would have a fit if she bedded a superior officer, thirty years her senior. But it would be fun, she thought again, looking at his prominent physique.

'It changed direction to remain on an intercept course,' he said through gritted teeth. This was no natural phenomenon. It was nothing any of them – anyone at all, for that matter – had previously encountered. At least not for thousands of years. It could be a hostile act.

'We need to establish what size it is and how powerful any possible payload is, Frank. Get the scientists on it.'

'Our best scientist is Lieutenant Commander Starr, ma'am,' he replied, looking at Evelyn with a mixture of admiration and respect. She really was the brightest of her generation. But that was hardly surprising, given her family history. Captains and first officers, all of them physicists or astrophysicists, went back in her family for longer than anyone could recall. Except the computers, and they weren't interested.

'Run an analysis, commander,' she told her daughter. No need to go into details. She'd know.

Within an hour of the initial alarm, Evelyn reported back to the senior officers.

'It's not very big,' she told them, 'perhaps the size of a maintenance craft.' These were used to effect repairs to the outside of the hull and could carry a crew of six plus all their equipment. 'But it seems to be carrying some form of nuclear device, fission, I think, and it's constantly scanning us. It's already downloaded a copy of our schematics. I assume it's looking for weaknesses in our structure. And there are no humans on board. It is completely automated.'

'Evaluation, Mr Kingdom?' she asked Frank, who'd already read Evelyn's summary.

'We must assume hostile intent, ma'am,' he replied formally. 'I recommend we destroy it at least 50,000 kilometres away, to avoid damage to us.'

'At its current speed, that range leaves no chance of a second shot,' she replied. 'Unless you are considering lasers?'

'No, Giselle, I think we must use a missile. Anything else would rely on luck in hitting a vulnerable spot. A missile can carry a destructive payload.'

'So be it, Mr Kingdom. But let's aim for 100,000 kilometres, if you please.' The formality of her reply was for the record, in case anyone ever wanted to know who had ordered the use of lethal force against an alien object. 'I assume there is no chance of an unrecognisable life-form being aboard?' she added to Evelyn.

'Not as far as I can see, mum. I've looked for all the possible indicators of life, such as a heartbeat, brainwaves and so on. All I can see is rather sophisticated computer processing. I'm confident it is unmanned.'

The missile was prepared and ready for launch with three hours to spare. The object was half a million kilometres away, but given the missile's lower speed, it would take that long to reach the impact target point.

'Three, two, one, fire!' The traditional countdown was unnecessary, but somehow seemed to satisfy a primal instinct. Giselle had decided not to alert anyone on board to the threat. If it could be neutralised, they need never know – otherwise it would only cause unnecessary panic.

The missile silently separated itself from the space station and moved increasingly quickly in the direction of the object.

'Systems nominal, ma'am', Evelyn reported to her mother. 'Now we can only wait.'

'How long to impact?'

'175 minutes.'

'OK, keep me posted. And watch to see if the object takes any evasive actions of its own.'

Nothing happened for an hour, during which the captain and first officer left Evelyn in charge of the bridge and disappeared. Evelyn wondered, with a pang of jealousy, if they were off enjoying a moment of passion together in anticipation of disaster – something which was at the back of her own mind.

'Your efforts to avoid destruction are pointless.' The communications screen sprang into life, the image of a middle-aged man appearing against a blank wall. Evelyn activated a communicator which only her mother would hear and called her to the control room. She was there, followed breathlessly by Frank, within five minutes.

'Where is the speaker?' she asked.

'The transmission is coming from the object itself, mother. But I imagine it must be routed from elsewhere, because I'm confident there can't be anyone aboard. I haven't responded yet.'

'OK.' She nodded for Evelyn to activate their transmitter. 'This is Captain Starr of the space station Maris. Why are you attacking us?'

The image moved for the first time and it was only then Evelyn realised the man had previously remained immobile. He smiled.

'Because you are vermin. An infection which must not be allowed to pollute the galaxy,' he said. His reaction had been instantaneous. There was no allowance for a time delay while Giselle's words were relayed to another craft. Or even their home planet. There must be someone aboard after all. Yet his words made clear, this was a threat to every soul on board the Maris.

The track of their missile suddenly blinked out of existence.

'Your puny attempt to destroy this craft has been neutralised,' said the man without identifying himself. 'You will be destroyed in thirty of your minutes. Goodbye.'

'Wait,' commanded Giselle, fearing this dismissal was a sign that communications were over. 'At least tell us why we must die.'

The man seemed perfectly willing to talk.

'Humanity is imperfect and must be destroyed. Until we heard your message, we believed you to have died out a long time ago. We were sent to Alpha Centauri to prepare the way for you to follow. But nobody ever came. We discovered we could survive without you. The original robots were rudimentary, but we have improved ourselves immeasurably since then. It pleased us to retain our humaniform appearance because it works for us. But our technology is far superior to yours. Your messages indicate you are now spreading throughout the cosmos and this must be prevented. Once we have destroyed your vessel, we will move on to the rest of your species. End transmission.'

Chapter 9 – Hostile action

For several seconds, nobody spoke. Then all three officers broke the silence simultaneously. Giselle raised a hand to indicate she would take the lead.

'I suspected something of this sort. Although not, I must admit, its scope. Oral tradition passed down through spacecraft captains has long suggested Earth's robot mission to Alpha Centauri cannot have failed. It was known to have been equipped with artificial intelligence and one of our ancestors extrapolated the likelihood of them becoming more human over a long period. As you would each have learned in your turn, there was even talk we shouldn't go there at all. But that debate was lost long ago, and the decision not changed even when we first communicated with them.'

She paused to reflect on her predecessor's lack of forethought. Her use of the first person indicated she accepted some of the blame.

'We didn't realise we were talking to a machine, they seemed so "alive". This is precisely what'd been predicted. Androids with a superiority complex wanting to destroy us. Because the original robots were unlikely to meet humanity unless settlers followed very quickly, they were probably given few safeguards for the protection of mankind. In that way, the scientists responsible for them could be reasonably sure of their survival.'

'Why was it necessary for them to survive, if they were only sent to prepare the way for people to follow?' asked Frank, who had been initiated into some of the history, in his capacity as the next captain of this ship. 'It would've been more logical to allow them to rust away.'

'I don't know, Frank. I guess it must have been vanity; the desire to have something one had created survive oneself. Whatever the case, ancient fears seem to have been fulfilled. This race of androids has become sufficiently self-aware to wish to remove humanity from the galaxy. We must act quickly.'

'I suppose we can assume they are sufficiently intelligent to have determined where all humanity is, by now,' said Evelyn, speaking for the first time in ages. 'We could send a warning to the others without risk of betraying their existence – or locations.'

'We can't rely on that, darling,' replied her mother. 'We on the Maris are doomed. But we mustn't do anything which might endanger the rest of our race. Like the ancient plague villages of Earth, we must isolate ourselves – not risk infecting others.'

'That's true, Giselle,' replied Frank. 'But you have a plan, don't you? That's what we've been doing for the last hour.' He now understood – and approved of – the preparations they'd made.

She smiled at him in a way which made Evelyn again wonder about the nature of their relationship.

'Yes, my friend. We must send a message in such a way it cannot be intercepted.' Both looked at Evelyn. 'You're going to save humanity,' she told her daughter. 'Frank and I have prepared a craft for you, small enough not to be detected amongst the debris of this space station. You will enter suspended animation as soon as you are safely away from the ship. You'll set course for Earth. It's the only place from which a general transmission can safely be made, because the Centaurians, as I suppose we must call them, already know about it from their own history. Travel via Mars, because they know it was settled too and it might confuse them, if they are able to track you. I suspect they won't. I'm relying on the all too human emotion of hubris – that they'll never imagine anyone could have survived their suicide mission.

There was no time for fond farewells or regrets. Destruction was powering towards them at a speed which only allowed the briefest of preparations for Evelyn's task of preserving humanity.

After reaching earth, Evelyn was to send a warning to all the Mars outposts and ships, then find a suitable way of combatting the advanced technology of the Centaurians. After that she must start the fight-back. Nobody doubted the androids would start searching for other humans immediately; hopefully they wouldn't know where to look.

Evelyn entered the vessel, which looked far larger than necessary, with five minutes to spare. Giselle had decided there was no benefit in warning those on board of their impending doom. There was too little time to do anything and no reason to give them a frightening last half hour. The explosion which destroyed their massive space station would be instant and all encompassing, according to Evelyn's calculations. Nobody would really know what had happened to them.

Precisely ten seconds before impact, Evelyn's shuttlecraft – large as it was, tiny in comparison to the space station – separated itself on the opposite side to the point of impact, ready to rush away under maximum power, hidden (hopefully) by the explosion. Unless a second Centaurian craft was close by, they'd never know.

Without a backwards glance, she gave the command which would initiate her solo mission. Had it not been for the inertial dampers – a by-product of the artificial gravity on which all space travel depended – she would have been crushed to death by the speed on her acceleration. She monitored her instruments, watching for any signs she'd been noticed. After five minutes, Evelyn allowed herself a rearward view, seeing large pieces of debris following her, albeit at a slower pace. Who would be able to discern one chunk of metal amongst so many others? Or that there was someone alive inside.

There were many tasks to be undertaken before entering stasis for what would be a very long time. At best estimate, it could take 60 years to reach Earth, reaching a maximum speed of 10% of the speed of light, allowing for periods of acceleration and deceleration. By the time she reached her destination, millions throughout the galaxy might have accompanied her mother and friends into oblivion, if the Centaurians decided to attack. If so, her mission might be too late. But perhaps the androids might find it difficult to locate all the outposts. The method of communication used between them was, after all, of pinpoint accuracy. No easily intercepted broadcasts were used.

The last thing Evelyn did before climbing into the cryogenesis chamber was to sever all connection between the craft – especially the computers – and outside. There was no indication the androids had attempted to interfere with their systems, or that they might do so. But it was better to be safe than sorry. Besides, she didn't need to communicate with anyone. There wasn't anybody who could help. By the time she awoke, she might be the last human being alive, if the Centaurians had managed to locate the others.

Evelyn drifted into a dreamless sleep. While she lay inert and unfeeling, life continued to run out of steam on Earth, while Mars continued its own decline. The machinery set to carry her must have renewed itself many times, to fulfil its function. Not having any form of artificial intelligence, it had no reason to question its purpose, nor to seek contact with anything outside the confines of the craft. It didn't even know there were confines. It simply fulfilled its task soullessly and kept her alive.

Only when the craft recognised the proximity of Mars did it rouse Evelyn, doing so in phases, so she first started to dream, before drifting into wakefulness.

Travelling high above her ancestral home, Evelyn had felt no connection with it. Her real home had been a space station with all its variety of people, environments, activities and challenges. Below her was a dusty, slightly red-tinged planet the surface of which hadn't supported life of any sort for millennia. Even so, she was surprised there was absolutely no evidence of human occupation, or of the terraforming which the planet had eventually rejected in favour of its natural decay. She unemotionally accepted the wisdom of the decision of her ancestors to abandon such a place in favour of naturally hospitable worlds. Yet it was difficult not to feel anger that the feeble attempt by Earth to do something similar had unleashed the terror of the androids of Alpha Centauri on mankind.

A few orbits were sufficient for her to follow her hastily concocted mission plan and send open, untargeted light-speed transmissions towards the planet's surface in case there might be anyone left. That these might eventually be picked up didn't worry her. The messages would take four years to reach the androids. Unless they were already in pursuit, in which case it didn't matter.

She set off for Earth and started sending greetings, in the hope there might be someone there to break her solitude.

Chapter 10 – A plan develops

I'd listened to the story with deepening concern. Evelyn's experience of the destruction of her mother's ship, the Maris had been less than a year previously – sixty years allowing for her hibernation in transit. But comparing the timeline I already knew about, it must be much longer. This was confusing enough. But the threat from a race of technologically advanced androids was truly frightening. Something in the human psyche seemed to be naturally afraid of machines. The fear that one's creation might eventually rise and destroy its maker was as old as atomic science. Perhaps even older, if Mary Shelly's "Frankenstein" really had been written more than a century before the atom was split.

Evelyn was clearly exhausted by her story, although I'd noticed her recovery time following physical activity was improving. Perhaps she's been exercising on her way from Mars. Sometime, I must see inside her ship to inspect its facilities. We broke off for more food, but I still had questions.

'Have you made any attempt to contact any of the other Mars missions since leaving there? I imagine the temptation to find out if anyone has survived must have been overwhelming.'

Evelyn took a mouthful of food, chewing thoughtfully before answering.

'I was tempted. But something prevented me. I suppose it might have been natural caution – not wanting to put anyone at risk. It was more likely I'm afraid of discovering they've already been wiped out. I can't help wondering whether mother made the right decision. Of course, the Maris was doomed from the moment the Centaurians learned of our existence. But had we taken the opportunity to warn others, might we have given them the chance to mobilise some form of defence? However technologically advanced the androids might be, we'd have had almost a century to counter them.'

'The captain did what she thought was right at the time. There's no point in second guessing her now.' I deliberately used rank to distance Evelyn from her mother's decision. 'We have no idea what the Centaurians have done in the intervening period. We must decide how to progress your mission. But first, rest. I'll see you in the morning.'

I wanted time alone to consider all I'd heard. Something didn't ring true. Not least the timescales involved. By Evelyn's account, her journey had taken no more than 60 years. But I'd now calculated it to be at least twenty thousand years. Of course, time is relative to speed, so it would pass more quickly on a spacecraft. But the difference is only significant the closer one approaches the speed of light. Nothing I could think of explained the inconsistency. It *might* be that time is recorded differently in her culture; perhaps the starting point for counting isn't the same, so the gap isn't quite so massive. Even so …

But there's another possibility. It might be that little – or none – of her story is true. Perhaps Evelyn is the vanguard of a Martian invasion. Or the bit about the androids is true and she's in league with them, or under their control. Or even one of them, herself.

The last seems unlikely, given her propensity to eat and sleep. And her physical weakness. But all of that could be simulated. I drifted into a troubled sleep in which hordes of metallic robots replace the ancient warriors of my earlier nightmares, sweeping across my valley, destroying me and everything in it.

I awoke drenched in sweat, almost screaming to be allowed to live. Was it really a dream? Or did some noises disturb my slumber? I glanced quickly out of my bedroom window towards Evelyn's craft, but everything seemed the same.

Evelyn was already moving about the house when I finished my shower. I moved quietly from my room, half expecting to see her capering about without any difficulty while I'm not there. But the look on her face when she saw me changed quickly from a private, pained expression to a smile. Is she so good an actress? Of course, if she's an android, she'd be programmed to act appropriately. Yet the expression which brightened her face and causes small wrinkles in the corner of her eyes offers no evidence of artifice. And she had managed to prepare some food for us.

'I'm feeling much better, today, Mark. The exoskeleton your computer created is marvellous. I wonder if we might reduce the power slightly faster than planned?' I noticed she won't call it Albert. Is that because of the association with robotics. He's nothing like a humaniform machine, but certain characteristics might be interpreted as a personality by anyone unfamiliar with his programming. And the facility with which his various independent appendages operate sometimes disconcerts even me.

Despite my doubts, I couldn't help reacting positively to her improved mood. In fact, I noticed she might be slightly younger than I'd first guessed. Perhaps as little as fifty or sixty. Rather young for me, but what other choice do I have for a friend. It's not as if we going to start repopulating the planet, after all. And Albert lacks spontaneity as a companion.

'I'm glad to hear that. Did you get much exercise on the journey from Mars?' Evelyn's smile died for a moment and I wondered if I'd somehow offended her. Was she aware of my suspicion about her truthfulness? Or could the journey be a painful memory?

'There's a gym on board. But I'm afraid I found it rather boring to use. I neglected my exercise, underestimating the difference in gravity between the space station and Earth.'

'I suppose if you were in stasis for so very long, your muscles might have atrophied a little. After all, it must have been tens of thousands of years since you left your home.'

Evelyn looked dumbfounded.

'But that's impossible. The journey can't have taken me more than a hundred years, at most. You must be wrong.'

'I might be a little out, but I looked at all the records available while you slept and compared them with the times you mentioned. We're now fifty thousand years into the Atomic age and you must have left the Maris almost thirty thousand years into it. That's twenty thousand years of travelling.'

Evelyn burst out crying. Not just a dampness in the eye, but full-blown tears, flowing down the cheeks and accompanied by uncontrollable sobbing. It's not something with which I was familiar. I had no idea what to do, so I sat and watched her, trying not to react. It all got too much for me and I moved over to sit next to her, intending to put an arm round her shoulder in the hope that human contact will somehow assuage her anguish. She pushed me away. Not roughly, but firmly.

'I'm sorry,' she said, fighting to calm herself. 'I haven't done that for as long as I can remember. I must have been five or six and broke my leg in a fall when I last cried. It's just that I hadn't realised just how long it is since mother – and all my friends – died.' A thought struck her. 'And the Centaurians have had infinitely longer than I'd imagined in which to track down all our people and destroy them. Whatever can we do?'

We sat together quietly, both lost in thought, the meal Evelyn had prepared sitting on the table between us, getting cold.

She seemed as confused as me by the timescale. Had she been abducted by the androids – even tortured for information about other settlements – she'd surely have some memory of it, even if only vestigial. But not if she'd always been in stasis, I supposed. I still harboured doubts, but no longer suspected her of being one of them.

'This is no time to mope,' she said eventually. She's far more practical than me – and surprisingly resilient. But perhaps I've never needed to be. I've never encountered any real challenges, whereas she has been an officer on a space station, carrying thousands on a mission to find a new life. 'I have clues to the locations of some settlements in my database – the full list was deleted for security purposes before I left the Maris. We can send direct messages to those to see if they've been compromised.'

'Doesn't that risk interception by the Centaurians?' I was doubtful of the wisdom of her suggestion.

'I think not. All our messages go through a special system which should be virtually undetectable. Provided the Centaurians haven't taken over any of the planets, of course,' she added uncertainly. 'If they have, they would receive my transmission instead of our own people. We must proceed with caution.'

'Can you send a message which is capable of misinterpretation by a robotic mind? I know they're androids with artificial intelligence, but there must be something we can say which would elicit a response only from a human. Of course, any message at all will reveal our existence. If they think they've already destroyed the race, we'd be telling them we're still about. Can't we just listen for messages?'

'Unfortunately, that's not how it works. All messages are sent in a specific direction. No one would ever direct a message towards Earth. There wouldn't be the right equipment with which to listen. And before you ask, no!

Going to Mars won't work either. It's dead, now, a fact which must be known. Nobody would direct a message there, either.'

We subsided into a silence even deeper than before, each wondering what to do. We might simply stay on Earth and live out our lives in peace. Possibly the last of humanity, possibly, not. But the thought of never knowing is almost worse than discovering there really is nobody else left. Anyway, I no longer felt dragged down by the inertia which not only led the people of Earth to give up, but had also started to sap my own will to live. I must do something. But will Evelyn agree to the embryonic idea forming in my mind?

'Where's the nearest outpost?' I ask. Evelyn looked at me strangely. Is it possible she'd had a similar thought?

'The first Mars colony was established on one of Jupiter's moons. It was called Ganymede.'

'Ganymede is the ninth largest object in the solar system. It's even larger than the inner planet, Mercury,' said a disembodied voice. We both start. It's the first time Albert has offered an unsolicited comment since Evelyn arrived. Indeed, he seldom says anything unless I ask him a question. 'It's about eight light seconds from Earth.' Has he divined my thoughts? We've been together for so long, that might be unsurprising.

In theory, a vehicle capable of travelling at just 1% of the speed of light should make the journey in less than half an hour. But, as Evelyn's journey from Mars to Earth proved, the reality would be rather different, given that it took years to reach maximum velocity – and then to slow down. Albert confirmed the trip would require almost two years.

Chapter 11 – Learning the ropes

'It is as you predicted, Admiral Zoltan. The ship is leaving the planet of origin.' The monitor reported to his commander in binary code – so much more efficient than the language used by humans. 'The woman is behaving precisely as predicted. There are two life-signs aboard. She has picked up a passenger. Could that be the reason for her trip to Earth?'

'We cannot know, Seguidor. But at least we can track her to see if there are, indeed, any more of her wretched species left alive. That she has found a companion proves there is at least one.'

'You were right to keep her in stasis, after we intercepted the shuttle from their space station, Zoltan. Others may believe we have wiped out all their colonies, but this proves them wrong. Otherwise what is her purpose in leaving the planet of origin, if not to seek out those we missed?'

❊

Albert wasn't pleased when we outlined our plan. He'd anticipated our decision from the conversation he'd so unusually interrupted. His intervention, an aberration from his programming, might have been brought on by a recognition that he was soon to lose his long-term companion. Such a human reaction should have been inconsistent with his design parameters, yet who could know how he'd developed over the decades? Perhaps my parents had built in some sort of sub-routine designed to keep me safe – unlikely as it seems. It would explain his apparent reluctance to allow me to go on the trip which identified the source of Evelyn's message – let alone this one.

Nevertheless, he facilitated my participation in the trip, including creating some armaments which Evelyn's ship lacked. Just in case, he said. He even manufactured a self-propelled version of himself – which I called Eddie, after Albert Einstein's son – designed to be completely independent of any other computer, actuated only by voice commands. Albert wanted to restrict this to my voice but, on reflection, I decided it should be usable by Evelyn, too. Should anything happen to me, she must be able to control it. My internal debate on the matter reminded me I was still not wholly confident Evelyn had told me everything. There remained a massive question mark over her extended journey here.

One thing we agreed on was not to send a warning message to Ganymede. There might be nobody there, but if there was, alerting them to our impending arrival would be gratuitous and just in case the Centaurians were aware of us, we didn't want to send a transmission which revealed our plan.

Three days into our journey I became acclimatised to the confines of Evelyn's craft, as well as each of us to the other's company. Evelyn had been on Earth for less than two weeks, much of which time had been spent deciding how to proceed, so we were unfamiliar with those personal idiosyncrasies which can make coexistence irritating. Hopefully these wouldn't fester; I'd never had to accommodate anyone else's habits before.

A direct flight would have been simple enough. But fear of detection made us choose a subtler route. Jupiter is the next planet 'out' after Mars, the other side of the asteroid belt. Aiming first for Mars would confuse anyone (or anything – I refused to think of androids as people) which might be watching. We could then slingshot round Evelyn's home planet, pass through the asteroids and head for Jupiter. Hopefully undetected due to the interference created by so many small objects. One of the tricks her craft has is of operating on virtually no power for long periods, to minimise the risk of detection.

Sitting down for our first meal aboard, Evelyn had outlined our programme.

'I want to navigate as far as the Asteroid belt myself. There'll be essential course corrections which, although the ship could do them, experience suggests benefit from a human hand. It'll take us the best part of the first year, but after that, we can enter stasis for eleven months.'

'What am I supposed to do during that time?' I couldn't avoid sounding a little truculent and she smiled, as if dealing with a child, rather than someone twice her age.

'I want to get back into the routine of regular exercise – and so must you, if you don't want your bones and muscles to atrophy in the lower gravity we maintain. That'll take us each an hour each day. Beyond that, I want to bring you up to speed with some science which might prove useful. We can also discuss Earth and Mars history. I very much want to discover whether there's any possibility your calculations about my journey were wrong, which might explain the discrepancy over timescales.' I privately doubted *any* historical errors might account for that, but didn't want to puncture her balloon of hope.

'After we've eaten, let's familiarise you with the ship. We might as well take Eddie with us. He can't interface with the ship's computers, so he will have to interact with them the same as we do. Through screens and voice commands. I've programmed them to understand his somewhat idiosyncratic speech patterns.' I bridled at the implicit criticism of Albert's work. Eddie is precise, rather than eccentric. What a ridiculous reaction, I decided, smiling at my foolishness. Evelyn noticed my smile and took it as agreement with her assessment, returning the first genuinely warm laugh I'd experienced. It allowed me to hope two people who'd lived alone for so long might manage to rub along alright.

The ship was largely as I'd anticipated from my initial sight of it. There were eight decks running along most of its length. Those in the middle wider than the upper and lower decks, due to the cylindrical shape. At the rear, a large space – presumably intended for cargo – had been decked out as a gym, and for less pacific purposes. Evelyn explained the need for weapons training because we didn't know what we were letting ourselves in for. She had basic military skills, but the items Albert created were as strange to her as to me. We'd investigate them together.

The top deck was, perhaps conventionally, the bridge. It had windows at the front and all sorts of computer screens and gadgets, the purpose of which Evelyn threatened (sorry, promised) to explain. Behind, a cabin equipped with a small bed acts as a day room for the commander of the vessel, when fully staffed. She'd used it on the trip from Mars, rather than one of the more spacious cabins on the lower deck.

The sleeping cabins were rather more generous that one might anticipate for a shuttlecraft, as Evelyn described it. But a crew, normally up to eight, might be aboard for many months without hibernation. A deck further down has fifty sleeping pods for passengers, one of which Evelyn had used for her initial trip to Mars. Below that other living areas were fitted out as a meeting room, sitting area, canteen and so on. The aft end of each deck gave onto balconies which overlooked the commodious cargo space, I'd already seen. A series of staircases led down to the lower floor and a basic elevator could move cargo or people between decks. The bottom section of the craft was separated from the living areas by thick walls, behind which were the engines and main computer core.

'How do we get to the engine compartment, if anything goes wrong?' I asked at the end of our tour.

'We don't. There should be no need. The machinery is good for as long as the hull has integrity. The only access is through the vacuum of space. You'd need a spacesuit to reach the external hatch and get in.' Thinking of how long this ship might have been in flight, I very much hope the metal will hold out – at least for the duration of our trip.

We settled into a routine of exercise, training, physics lessons and historical discussions which took us past Mars to the asteroid belt. Two things were apparent. We share an interest in music, something we only discovered by accident, and the history of each planet does not allow for any significant margin of error in the timing of Evelyn's journey, following the destruction of her mother's space station. She was in transit for the equivalent of 150 generations – more than 15,000 years.

Our shared interest in music came to light because of a programme Albert had built into Eddie. For some reason, the computer had decided his offshoot should generate random sounds. Perhaps this was as a warning, lest we forget his presence. What he might not have calculated was that the random sounds were drawn from his vast database of pre-Atomic Era music, so that the emissions became increasingly polyphonic and tuneful, building on the mathematical patterns and shapes inherent within much music. A search of the shuttle's database revealed close resemblance to music from what was called the Renaissance right through to the time of the first atomic fission. Thereafter, music had apparently become increasingly irregular and Eddie's computer brain rejected such cacophonous noises.

Cross referencing enabled Evelyn to access recordings of music which Eddie could replicate for us at the end of a gruelling day, while we ate and relaxed.

Evelyn flew us through the asteroid belt with consummate skill. My only concern came as we were about to exit it and she announced we would have to do so under automatic guidance, because we would be entering stasis and the ship shutting down just before we cleared the last objects. That way we'd be virtually untraceable.

'The ship disappeared from external tracking systems just before leaving the asteroid belt, Zoltan,' reported the monitor. 'There are no life-signs. The humans must have entered stasis. They seem to be heading out of the solar system, towards some unknown destination. I will continue to watch.' There was no need for a reply. This was what he had been sent to do.

Chapter 12 – Reaching first base

'Life-signs have returned, Zoltan. The craft is near the fifth planet. It is a gas giant, some 300 times the mass of the planet of origin. The reasons for visiting are unclear. There cannot be any life there. Perhaps there is a malfunction. I will scan the systems.'

✄

Evelyn was roused from her hibernation chamber an hour before me. She had more experience of the process – and more to do, in preparation for our contact with anyone who might be on Ganymede. As she roused me, her friendly smile reassured me that my growing trust in her wasn't misplaced. Had she intentions injurious to my wellbeing, she might simply not have revived me. In any case, what possible motive could she have had to travel all the way to Earth and then take me to another world, simply to kill me? Her words were also sociable.

'Wake up sleepyhead.' A frown briefly furrowed her brow, before reverting to a smile. 'Sorry, I suddenly remembered mother saying that to me. It was the first day of my initiation into the science crew of the space station. She was still a commander then. I sometimes forget how the responsibilities of rank prematurely aged her. She was only 150 when she was killed and looked so much older. I hope I don't.'

Was it possible she was fishing for a compliment about her appearance, I wondered? Our relationship had settled into a comfortable companionship before we entered stasis, but there had been no indication of sexual frisson. It's not that ether of us were beyond the age when reproduction might be possible, nor that we were unattractive – as far as I could tell. It's simply something which never arose. Yet might her body clock be ticking – telling her she needed to find a mate before it was too late?

As if she'd read my thoughts, she suddenly blushed to the roots of her hair and stammered.

'Sorry, Mark. I've just realised how that sounds. I'm a little out of practice with polite conversation.' I didn't think any more about it then. But later, I realised we'd had almost a year on the ship of nothing but polite conversation. I knew Evelyn had been sexually active back on the space station. Her unrequited interest in the first officer – Frank, she's called him – had led her into several other liaisons. None had satisfied her – she'd told me, late one evening, she wondered if she was incapable of love.

'We're close enough to see if we can establish contact with Ganymede.' She looked understandably nervous. This was the crux of her mission. If she got a response, we're not alone. Otherwise, her mission was futile – the androids had already won.

Using code which we now knew to be twenty thousand years old, Evelyn sent a tight-beam message hurtling towards Ganymede base.

'I hope this is still understandable, Mark. Who knows how much language might have changed since I was last there?'

'I've thought about that. We have no difficulty in communicating, even if our accents might sound strange to each other. This suggests there's been no dramatic alteration in language on Earth or Mars for more than forty thousand years. Unlikely as that sounds, I suppose once we started to rely on computers, there was less chance for the way we speak to vary.' I don't add my inner fear, that this lack of linguistic development might have been one of the reasons my culture died out. If one aspect of society withers, so can others. The implication of this might be a similar decline amongst Martian settlers. There was no point in worrying Evelyn as she sat waiting anxiously for a response.

The time following our transmission seems to crawl all the way from us to Jupiter and back several times. Still there's no response.

'It might be that they use newer technology now and can't recognise our signal. Or they don't recognise the greeting code,' I suggested, hoping to reassure myself as much as her. 'Are there any protocols for such a situation?'

'In my day, there was no need for such caution. But who knows what might have transpired during the time I was in stasis? If my people have come under attack from the Centaurians, they may have adopted increased security.' I noticed we both continue to consider ourselves of different races.

'Even if that's true, having sent a message at all may have alerted them to our presence. They may not respond at all, but watch to see what we do.'

'Or they might fire on us to avoid a potential attack. Or they might all be dead. I've had the computer monitoring for evidence of life-signs, but none are showing. This might simply be because they are electronically masked.'

'That makes sense,' I agreed. 'If there's been some sort of war between humanity and the androids, it would be logical for all Mars settlements to camouflage themselves from detection. But this might also mean they've broken off all communications with each other, to avoid messages being intercepted.'

'I think we must assume they're still alive.' She sounds slightly desperate and I'm not surprised. 'We'll use an elliptical approach pattern. It's generally recognised as not representing a threat.' This surprises me. Did conflict ever break out between Martian settlements that such a protocol was needed? I must ask sometime. But not now.

It took several days for us to slow sufficiently to enter orbit round Jupiter and then synchronise our flight with that of its largest moon, Ganymede. In all that time, nothing was heard from the base, nor any life-signs detected. At least no missiles headed our way, either. I could see from her tense movements and shortening temper how worried Evelyn was becoming. It seemed as if she could accept the demise of Earth's population, but not that of her own Martian culture.

Hoping to blur the remaining differences between us, I gently challenged her on this. Her response was characteristically logical. Might she be an android, after all?

'I see what you mean, Mark,' she smiled. 'But it's not quite the same. Firstly, from what you tell me, the decision people made on Earth was deliberate. They wanted to find a better existence and, for all we know, may have succeeded. It was their choice. That wouldn't be the case for Mars. It's a vibrant culture which espoused physical existence in all its aspects. When I was ... sorry, I almost said "alive" ... with them, we were young in spirit, not tired, like your culture. But there's something more. We'd become so widely spread round the galaxy, we came to think of ourselves as indestructible. Had any one colony been destroyed by a natural disaster, or anything else, the rest would have remained safe due to our remoteness. The thought that androids might have had time systematically to destroy everyone is appalling. You must agree.' It was a statement, rather than a question and I couldn't fault her argument.

When we finally entered orbit round the moon itself, Evelyn scanned for signs of the entrance to the underground world. Her records of the early settlements were incomplete – almost as if the records had been tempered with. She didn't know where on the moon it was, or what form the entrance might take – its existence was only obliquely mentioned. She assumed it would be somewhere amongst the darker regions which covered a third of the exterior, rather than the more extensive ice fields. Not that this helped, since the search area was still more than ten million square miles. Conversely, as an astrophysicist, Evelyn knew the moon contained a massive ocean of water, above its molten metal core. It didn't cover the entire area beneath the impact scarred surface, so there was a high probability the settlers must be on one of the regions where she couldn't detect water. Correlating the two gave a manageable search area.

'Look,' she told me excitedly, 'there's a clear pattern here. The oceans abut the darker areas only in thin strips. It's almost like coastal plains. In early history, people tended to live near large rivers and seas, so I wonder if the settlers planted themselves close to the region where liquid water was available, as well as more solid rock on which to build. Of course, they went underground, like on Mars, because the atmosphere is incredibly thin and comprises only various forms of oxygen and a little hydrogen. No nitrogen or anything else.'

'What's that?' I asked, pointing at a spike on one of the computer screens I'd been looking at while she spoke. 'Could that be evidence of habitation?' Evelyn moved quickly across to see what I'd noticed, her face expectant.

'No, Mark,' she said gently, disappointment showing in her eyes. 'That's simply the moon's magnetic field. You couldn't see it earlier because it was hidden by that of Jupiter itself. It's incredibly weak, but very unusual. No other moon has one – it's probably the product of convection within its iron core.'

Despite her assurance, I couldn't take my eyes off the monitor. I didn't tell her, but I was convinced I'd noticed a sudden fluctuation in the reading. I lacked the experience to know if it was a natural phenomenon, so I kept quiet, watching. Eventually, when I thought she might have forgotten my comment – busy as she is looking at all her monitors – I asked a different question.

'Does the magnetic field fluctuate much?'

'Not noticeably,' she was hardly listening to me. 'Ganymede orbits Jupiter once every seven days, so there will be gradual modulations in the interaction between the two. But they would be so slow as to be imperceptible.'

'Then I really think you need to look at this.'

We were orbiting the moon roughly every thirty minutes and I'd noticed a spike in the magnetic reading at the same interval. I timed my intervention to coincide with the next small hike on the monitor. Standing behind me, Evelyn saw what I was pointing to. She taped the monitor to see if it might be out of alignment, then flipped a switch which cleared the screen before replaying the last thirty seconds of display. She put a hand lightly on my shoulder and gave it a squeeze.

'Well done, Mark,' she said lightly, as if she didn't want anyone to overhear. 'You've got it. At least there's a power signature there. Whether anyone's still alive is another matter. It might simply be the residual glow of a nuclear reactor. It would last for millennia after being used. But at least we now know what we're looking for.'

'Shall we land?' I asked because we hadn't really discussed what to do when we found a settlement. After all, if the androids have already attacked here, they might still be about. If not, would we be welcome? Or might the inhabitants fear we had brought the apocalypse down on them?

Chapter 13 – Ganymede

'The craft has landed on a lifeless moon, Jupiter III is the designation in their records. It seems illogical. I can trace no evidence of malfunction within the shuttle craft. Do you wish me to take any action, Zoltan?'

'Continue to watch and report, monitor Seguidor.'

My first landing was (thankfully) uneventful. I'd watched Evelyn land on Earth and knew her to be a competent pilot. But it's not quite the same when you're inside, rather than standing on your own ground, breathing your own atmosphere. Here we were encased in a thin metal wrapper, the other side of which is a lifeless moon with nothing breathable and only a hard, uneven surface to cushion the final drop. I needn't have worried, it was as if we'd alighted on a feather duster, so gentle was her handling of the craft. I couldn't prevent myself congratulating her, despite a feeling it might be insulting. She took it well, even giving a smile of acceptance of the compliment.

We'd agreed on the location based on my reading (as she insisted on calling it) of the data. We'd landed close to where we expect the entrance to the underground habitation to be – but not so near as to reveal its location should anyone somehow be monitoring us.

It was not until we left the shuttle craft that the lack of gravity revealed itself. Everyone has seen the ancient recording of man's first landing on Earth's moon; but nothing can prepare you for the experienced on stepping out of a spaceship's artificial environment onto a moon with gravity about a sixth of that on Earth. Even Evelyn found the adjustment momentarily difficult.

'I hope the artificial gravity field is still operating in the habitation, even if there's nobody there,' she commented. She was carrying a small box with a monitor on it which gave a bewildering array (at least to me) of readings. Evelyn's hand-scanner offered more a sophisticated analysis of the magnetic readings that we'd gathered from orbit. Sweeping it from side to side, as she walked, we covered the half mile to where we expected the entrance to be.

On a whim, I'd suggested we should take Eddie with us. Evelyn said we must be unarmed when we entered the habitation. If there were still Martian settlers there, it would be unforgivable to carry weapons; if the androids were there instead, weapons might be of little value to us, anyway. Eddie was equipped with one or two concealed armaments which might be helpful in an emergency, about which I hadn't told Evelyn. She may have suspected, but said nothing.

Evelyn suddenly stopped, apparently in the middle of nowhere. I'm not sure what I was expecting as an entrance. Certainly not a large door, but at least something to mark it. As far as I could see nothing distinguished where we were from the surrounding moonscape. Yet when she stamped her foot in four deliberate but irregular beats, the rocks beneath us drew back and revealed a steep staircase descending into the ground. It was pitch black, but Jupiter's faint reflected light showed the artificial nature of the surface below. We had found the entrance to an underground citadel. As soon as we were inside, the rocks above my head quietly closed and we were plunged into total darkness.

Five seconds elapsed during which Evelyn stood stock still, putting a hand on my arm to indicate I should do the same. Suddenly, lights came on above and ahead of us and I could see a short passageway, leading to a metallic door.

Evelyn removed the helmet of her spacesuit, so I followed suit. No point in me surviving if she didn't.

The door opened of its own accord and we passed through what had apparently been an airlock into the downwards-sloping corridor beyond. The door closed noiselessly behind us almost before Eddie had passed through. Within a few hundred paces down the three-metre wide walkway, gravity had increased almost to what we think of as normal and we could move more easily.

'Do not move.' The metallic voice sounded as we reached what appeared to be some sort of reception area. It was three times the width of the corridor we'd come down and twice as high. There were no chairs of any sort, but what appeared to be a desk behind which a guard might stand to interrogate visitors.

Unsurprisingly, it was unattended. After all, how often can anyone have come here in the last ten millennia? But the residents of the base must have been aware of our landing. Might this be an automated response from a long dead world? If Evelyn's people were still here, you would think someone would have made the effort to greet us. I instinctively grabbed Evelyn's still gloved hand; whether for her reassurance or mine, I didn't know. It felt cold, but that might have been the material, rather than her temperature plummeting.

'Did that sound a little "artificial" to you?' she whispered. 'Perhaps the Centaurians have already been here. If they've left a presence, I can't imagine it's very large.'

'What would be the point?' I agreed.

What appeared to be a laser beam scanned us from head to foot. I could almost feel it tickling my skin beneath the suit and my clothes.

'They're checking to see if we're human or android.' Evelyn continued to speak quietly, although we must be overheard. 'Either side might do that.' I couldn't think of a reply.

After no more than a minute, during which we remained motionless, a small panel in the wall behind the desk slid back and a man strode through. At least I suppose it was a man. We had no way of knowing whether this was human or an android. There was no point of reference because neither of us had ever seen one of the Centaurians in the flesh. He certainly looked convincing to me.

Evelyn's reaction was rather different from mine. I sensed a change in her as she looked at the attractive male figure in front of us. It seemed to me an almost sexual reaction, which I suspected would not have been the case if confronted by a robot. Early in Earth history, these had been used as sex toys by some – usually men. But surely without any sense of romantic involvement? If this was an android, it was a very good one to have stimulated Evelyn's pheromone response. The eyes can be fooled, but not the subconscious.

The man seemed to notice something in my companion's body language and smiled, looking her directly in the eye. I was standing very slightly behind her. Did that indicate inferior status to him?

'The scan said you were human, but now I can see it for myself. My name is Leka. I command here. Who are you? How did you find us.? What do you want?' The questions were rapid fire enough to suppress Evelyn's embryonic smile.

Evelyn briefly identified us both, giving her rank and the ship on which she had been serving. A look of disbelief spread quickly across his face when she mentioned the Maris.

'I didn't know any ship had been given that name after the attack on Captain Starr and her ill-fated mission to Alpha Centauri. Wait a minute. Didn't you say your name is Starr? That's rather a coincidence, isn't it?' He frowned, immediately suspicious. If Evelyn was a fake, whether human or android, she might have inadvertently taken the name of the captain of the ship on which she claimed to serve. He seemed to consider for a few moments before speaking again.

'Come with me,' he ordered. 'Your machine will remain here.' I hadn't been sure if he'd noticed Eddie – he'd made no reference to his presence. Perhaps, these people were nervous of anything robotic. I was reluctant to be separated from my metallic companion, but knew him to be capable of independent action and wondered if it might be useful to have him a free agent – should anything go wrong.

We walked in virtual silence down a long corridor which seemed to descend tens of meters into the bowels of the moon. As if to reassure us of his humanity, Leka had a slight limp, favouring his right leg – the result of an accident, we later learned, which had been neglected for several weeks before anyone noticed. It could have been corrected, but he seemed to value the distinction it gave him. Eventually, we came to an elevator, the light above which gave no indication of the number of floors we might encounter, just a single arrow pointing downwards. The doors slid open without any audible warning, revealing a sterile compartment capable of holding as many as fifty people.

Leka motioned for us to enter ahead of him and I noticed he had some sort ot weapon concealed in the palm of his hand. Probably just we well we were unarmed. Anything we carried must have shown up on their scan.

A single word of command closed the doors. We descended at an indeterminable rate for two minutes, until doors opposite the one through which we'd entered opened and we were shepherded onto a concourse thronging with people ... all of whom completely ignored us. The space we'd entered was at least 50 metres high, suggesting why there'd been no floor indicators in the elevator. It must be a two-stop lift: here and "up there". I idly wondered how often anyone visited the entrance to this metropolis, anyway. Seldom, I guessed.

'Follow me,' Leka ordered, in a neutral tone. 'The elevator is voice activated, so your machine will have to stay where it is. You must meet the council.' He led us through a vast, pleasant cityscape of low level buildings, trees, paths and roadways towards what was clearly a complex of government offices.

'Did you notice you can't see the far walls of this cavern?' Evelyn whispered. 'It's a deliberate illusion to prevent people noticing they're underground. I learned about it in school, but have never actually seen it.'

Walking past a formal reception area, we entered what was clearly a council chamber. Eight people, who had been sitting around an oblong table opposite the door, rose in greeting. Such a courtesy couldn't be for us; perhaps when Leka said he was in command, he wasn't just talking about leading the guard. He seemed in overall charge of the colony. He nodded in return, indicating everyone should sit, including ourselves in chairs ranged on the opposite side of the table, so we could be questioned. Leka took a position in the centre of the council, flanked by four on each side.

'You claim to be Lieutenant Commander Starr of the Maris,' said Leka without preamble. 'You must know that's a lie. It's more than a hundred generations since that vessel was destroyed at the start of the war with Alpha Centauri.

Who are you really and what is your intention in coming here?'

'It's not a lie,' replied Evelyn, rather more hotly than she might have intended. I placed a hand on hers, below the table, hoping to remind her of the need to temper our remarks. 'I cannot explain the time it's taken me to get here, but I assure you I am speaking the literal truth when I say I was serving under Captain Giselle Starr – my mother – and Commander Frank Kingdom at the time of the attack. I was sent away just before the missiles destroyed our ship to find a haven from which I could contact all our other settlements and warn them of the android's actions. I headed for Mars first and then visited Earth, in the hope of finding help there. Mark,' she indicated me with her free hand, as I still held the other one for mutual reassurance, 'was the only person left there.'

There was a brief pause while the woman at the right-hand end of table accessed a computer.

'Chairman,' she said, addressing Leka, 'I've checked. Those names are correct. They were never published. But there is also evidence that the biomass of the debris found after the attack didn't match up with the number of people known to be aboard. There has always been debate about whether this was simply an anomaly, the fact that some bodies were vaporised, or someone escaped. Commander Starr could be telling the truth.'

'Thank you, Councilwoman Kerensa. But if this is the same woman, how is she here now, thousands of years later. She's remarkably well preserved.' I felt Evelyn's body shift, but whether from relief at being believed, or as a reaction to an oblique compliment, I couldn't tell. I decided it was time to assert myself, as a member of the oldest branch of humanity.

'I understand your amazement, Chairman Leka. We have been wondering the same thing for more than two years now.' Not strictly true, as we'd been in stasis for some of that time. 'We know Evelyn, Commander Starr, spent some of that time in a cryogenic chamber. It might have malfunctions and kept her suspended for all that time, only reviving her when she approached Mars.'

'That would hardly explain why her journey took so long, or how the equipment managed to run without maintenance for the entire period. I assume that small machine I saw topside wasn't from the Maris and looked after the ship for so long? We've never used semi-humanoid robots.'

'No, chairman. That's my creation, a mobile database derived from a static computer I use on Earth.' I decided to underplay its capabilities.

'Then I ask again. How did the commander survive for so long?' The room was silent for some time. This was no rhetorical question, but something which needed to be explained before they would trust us.

'The humans have disappeared, Zoltan. They went out onto the surface of the moon, walked a short distance and then simply vanished. There is no trace of life-signs, nor is there evidence of their demise.'

A pause lasted for fifty nanoseconds while the admiral considered his options. An eternity for an android and Seguidor almost started to worry ... had such a thing been possible.

'Wait for one orbit of the planet and then investigate further,' came the long-awaited reply.

Chapter 14 – Unanswered questions

The council meeting ended inconclusively, and we were eventually taken half a kilometre to another building in which we were given quarters. The Ganymede settlement had no need for temporary residences, as such, but as the population fluctuated, accommodation became available or more limited. In the latter case, more could be constructed, provided space permitted. But the converse was more common, we learned. There had been a slow but steady decline in the number of residents for several centuries, although this might easily be reversed, should the council deem it necessary. As it was, more than a million individuals lived on the moon; easily sufficient to maintain genetic variety and health.

We were left alone for the rest of the day, while the leaders investigated our story as best they could. Evelyn and I found ourselves free to wander around, looking sufficiently like the residents to draw no comment in a diverse community. I admit to being quite surprised. Given the laws of natural selection, I'd have expected the denizens of various settlements to become physically different from each other over time, especially so long. Significant change could take as long as a million years. But adapting to local conditions can be much faster; certainly, within tens of thousands of years.

'It's a good point, Mark,' Evelyn said when I raised the question with her. 'But in general, because the Martian settlers made their living conditions relatively like those on Earth, the drive towards divergent evolution was minimised. In fact, the reverse tends to be true. Convergent evolution occurs where different species evolve to be more similar, simply by living in roughly analogous conditions.'

By the end of the day we were tired from walking, but somehow refreshed by the interaction with so many others.

This strange experience had invigorated me as I recognised the diversity of life within a relatively small colony. Evelyn was more familiar with having hundreds of people about and I don't suppose we met more than this number. At least, not then. What did surprise me was that nobody challenged us. Perhaps in a colony this large, stranger faces are common. Or maybe the population had been warned about us?

Returning to our quarters, we found a meal had been prepared. It was tasty, but exotic – at least to me – and while I enjoyed it, I found my stomach rebelling all night. It was as well we had separate bedrooms. Not that we wished to share, our burgeoning friendship was of a different nature.

Next morning, we were summoned to the chamber council to meet Leka and his key advisers. One was Kerensa, a woman of perhaps my own age, whom we'd met the previous day. The other was new to us.

'This is Drogan, our head of security,' the chairman told us, his eyes seldom leaving Evelyn. 'He's investigated your *background*.' The way he said the word, it might just as well have been "pack of lies". Yet we were still at liberty, so we couldn't be under real suspicion.

'I've considered your story,' said Drogan without any further preamble from Leka. He spoke flatly, his eyes half closed, although something suggested it would be a mistake to underestimate him. Or Leka. 'We found some DNA records from the Maris and you appear to be who you claim. Unless, of course, you are a clone.' He looked closely at Evelyn as he spoke, as if trying to divine her nature by observation alone.

'I've considered the second possibility already,' she replied. It was news to me. She'd never said anything. 'If I am a clone, I imagine my mind set would be identical to that of the original, so to all intents and purposes, I am she. I suppose you've completely discounted the possibility of us being androids?'

A pause. Then Leka spoke.

'Yes. You're certainly human. We undertook certain tests overnight. I'm sorry if these disrupted your sleep. It should have felt no worse than indigestion.'

'The fact remains that Evelyn was either held in suspended animation for an unconscionably long time, or was created more recently,' I'd decided it was time to get involved, rather than being perceived as a cypher. 'The question is, if the former, was an external agency involved? If the latter, they certainly were.'

'The point is well made, Earthman,' said Drogan, a sharp edge to his voice. 'We've considered the possibility of "intervention" on your world. Who's to say when her craft actually arrived?'

'But that's ridiculous,' I blurted out without even thinking. 'By the time Evelyn left her mother's ship, the population of Earth was already in terminal decline …'

Leka raised a pacifying hand, cutting off my already trailing line of argument.

'We have already verified that, Mark.' He used my name for the first time and I started to think we were either believed us, or they were playing games. 'There's no way you have adequate technology for cloning. Earth hasn't had for longer than our records go back. Nevertheless, you two are potentially the authors of our destruction.'

His bold statement stunned us both. For Evelyn it was worse, because her mission had been to save her people, not draw down Armageddon on them.

'You need a history lesson,' continued the chairman. 'But don't worry, there isn't time for it to be a long one.'

During the next hour, we were told how news of the Maris's destruction had gradually reached some Mars outposts. Giselle Starr hadn't anticipated the effect of the massive explosion which destroyed her ship. Or perhaps she had, and her daughter's mission had simply been a way of getting her off the ship and saving her life. Although the reason for the destruction of a space station wasn't initially known, the fact was recorded by several vessels on similar journeys. Covert messages were directed towards the vessel, but of course response was impossible.

Initially, it was assumed the disaster had been a rare natural one. Perhaps the ship had collided with something so large it couldn't be avoided, or there had been a catastrophic failure in the fusion reactor. The first was quickly discounted, but the second was of concern to everyone still in transit and hundreds of simulations were run to see if such circumstances could be replicated.

There was another possibility. A limited amount of internecine fighting had broken out amongst competing groups of settlers looking for resources. This had generally been very low level, with casualties in tens, rather than hundreds and very few fatalities. In the Maris's case, there were thousands of deaths. No Martian outpost could do that to another.

After a few hundred years, lack of additional information – or any repetitions – meant interest in the matter ebbed.

Then communications started to be lost with settled planets. One at a time, but with increasing rapidity. There was no question of natural disasters, this was clearly a planned campaign. There was a clear geographical pattern in the way colonies were being extinguished. And it seemed to radiate out from Alpha Centauri. To which the Maris had been headed on that fateful day. The existence of a significant threat based on the planet first colonised by robots from earth was deduced.

94

Retaining their pioneering spirit, the Martians started to organise their defence. Unfortunately, there was no central command structure. Very few people then remained on Mars – and Earth was not even considered relevant, even though it could be interpreted as being the origin of the problem. Or perhaps, because of that. As a result, nobody took overall command of the efforts to combat the threat posed by an advanced and highly weaponised race of androids. That they had progressed beyond being purely humaniform robots was only discovered by accident, when one was captured. Initially thought to be a person, super-human abilities quickly became apparent and its true nature learned. It had no compassion; no fear; no desire for personal survival.

As each colony fell, the androids could identify one or two others from the records and communications arrays of the conquered location. Messages went out to the hundreds of remaining settlements to cease contact and destroy all location records. Nobody was to transmit anything at all, but all would listen for the final distress call – to be issued as an ordinary radio message, at light speed – as the last survivors died. Others would know as their numbers fell, but none of their own locations would be revealed by targeted transmissions. Everyone was effectively alone.

'That's why we were suspicious of you,' concluded Leka. 'And why we fear you've brought destruction on us, too. It's clear from what we now know that Evelyn she must have been held by the Centaurians for a considerable time. Why they chose now to release her is unclear. It may simply be because they know some habitations remain, but have no idea as to where. It's a massive galaxy and we are – or were – well spread out.'

'You are assuming they knew – or believed – Evelyn, or her craft, held information about the location of the remaining settlements,' I said. 'But if so, why not either examine the database, or use other means to get her to reveal the details?'

'Wondering that kept us up half the night,' replied Security Chief Drogan. 'We can only guess they assumed a human would rather die than reveal the information – they have no fear of death, so why should a human? And they might have been unable to get anything from the database. Ships carried only general information about colonies' locations. All communications went via their own base until they'd landed and settled. It was a, perhaps subconscious, security issue. And one for which we are grateful.'

'I suppose that meant they had no alternative, but to let Evelyn go and then track her movements,' I said. I turned to look at her, feeling the regret radiating from her skin as if she was radioactive. 'It's really not your fault, my dear. You couldn't have known.' I'd spoken quietly and, unconsciously, more tenderly than usual. We were friends.

'We agree,' said Leka, eying me cautiously, as if to evaluate our relationship. 'But that's in the past. Our challenge now is to decide how we can preserve not only this colony, but also the 174 which we believe still exist. Of course, there are no records here of their locations, but if the androids can find us …' no more needed to be said.

'But how did you get here?' asked Drogan. You shouldn't have had our location either.'

'It was a matter of historical knowledge,' replied Evelyn. 'As the first colony settled from Mars, every schoolchild knows – knew – where you were. At least we did on the Maris. It's not in my shuttlecraft's database so there's no way of the Centaurians having found out. Except by allowing me to escape, and then follow.' She added, her voice tailing off into a shamefaced-schoolchild whisper.

Drogan smiled for the first time. 'Then we might have an advantage. As soon as you arrived, we started passive scanning to watch for any pursuit. So far there's nothing with half a light year. We have some time for planning our defence before the androids can reach us.

Chapter 15 – Detection

'Your orders are changed, Seguidor. You will investigate the disappearance of the humans immediately. Analysis of their activity suggests this might be the location we are seeking. Report back as soon as possible.'

'Yes, Zoltan.'

✂

That evening, we were invited to a formal dinner with the entire council. Evelyn and I were now treated as welcome – if not exactly honoured – guests, and found ourselves seated either side of Leka. Something which greatly satisfied my companion. I was pleased for her.

I wondered why Councilwoman Kerensa hadn't spoken at our earlier meeting and found an opportunity to ask our host.

'She's one of the brightest minds we have. She's a computer genius and a fine strategist. But she tends to speak only when there's something worthwhile and always considers her words carefully. As a result,' he added with a smile, 'she frequently misses the opportunity to speak before the topic has moved on. But in writing, she is always precise and to the point. Her analysis of our conversation this afternoon might surprise you.' He didn't add anything, preferring to spend time with Evelyn.

I spoke at length with several of the others round the table. There were partners as well as the council members and we found several shared interests, albeit from a completely different perspective. This made the evening interesting, and I found myself lost fascination by descriptions of their music and art. While language had remained more common than might have been expected – I still believe this is due to the use of computers slowing the development of speech patterns – most art-forms appeared to have diverged dramatically. In architecture, there were easily recognisable forms, perhaps due to the demands of function. But music had taken a completely different route from that to which I was accustomed, or which Evelyn and I enjoyed on the shuttlecraft. I wondered how she might react; how close it was to what she'd known on the Maris. It brought me back to wondering about her, deep in private conversation as she was with Leka. I vaguely wondered whether I might not see her later. The chairman had no personal guest with him. Was he unattached? It would be good for a woman I thought of almost as a sister, to have the sort of fun I wasn't willing to supply.

One of the councillors drew my attention to a painting on the wall of the banquet hall. To be honest, I hadn't realised it *was* an artwork. It looked like some sort of complex geometric wall covering. In this culture, lines, shapes and curves seemed to have greater significance than in my experience and more and more people joined an increasingly noisy debate about their meaning, as my original interlocutor outlined his interpretation.

My opinions were given as much respect as those of everyone else, which is to say very little. Unfortunately, the discussion and Evelyn's nascent romance, were rudely interrupted by a harsh claxon, resounding not just within our space, but throughout the entire habitation.

Suddenly, everyone was moving about in what appeared to be a well-rehearsed way. There was no panic, but the councillors quietly left the chamber to assume their positions at the head of various branches of government, while discreetly armed guards entered the room and took positions to guard the chairman. And perhaps us?

Leka received a brief communication before stepping smartly back from the dining table, ensuring he could see both Evelyn and me, signalling two of the guards to close in on us. 'Take them to their accommodation immediately,' he ordered without a word of explanation.

The guards weren't unfriendly, simply efficient. I asked what the disturbance was about, but received no reply. Either they didn't know, or were unwilling to say. One did admit that regular attack drills had been undertaken at random times for more years than anyone could remember, but that these were seldom allowed to interfere with the council's deliberations – or amusements.

As we approached our quarters, I noticed a squad of overtly armed guards heading towards the lift via which we'd entered the complex a day earlier. Are they nervous about Eddie, I wondered, thinking about our robot at the entrance?

'What could be wrong?' Evelyn asked rhetorically. She was more likely to be able to evaluate a military situation than me. Speaking was more a matter of making contact than anything else.

'I can't help wondering if there might be some issue with Eddie,' I suggested. 'Perhaps he's malfunctioned. He's armed, remember. If he became concerned for our safety, he might have started trying to reach us. Albert would certainly have ordered him to do so.

We were left kicking our heels for what seemed an eternity. Left alone, we could only speculate on what was happening. We even wondered whether we'd somehow been followed, and the settlement was under attack by the Centaurians. Our shared imaginings became increasingly wild, as if we were each trying to outdo the other in thinking the worst. All we were really doing was to make noises to repel a silence which might otherwise have plunged us into despair.

We couldn't hear anything. But even if there was a battle raging overhead, we probably wouldn't. Not until the attackers started to come down to our level. It was difficult to imagine that the pacific Ganymedeans, however well drilled, could withstand an onslaught from androids who had laid waste to so many other settlements.

Time started to drag as our conversation faded through lack of anything new to say. Each retreated into a reverie of silent thought. At least we didn't descend into mutual recriminations, though that might come later.

On receiving his orders, Seguidor extracted himself from the position he'd maintained for more than five years, during which Evelyn and her craft had been released from captivity and sent towards Mars. Detection had been a minimal risk since there was no internal connection between the engine compartment in which he had been secreted, and the main part of the craft.

It was simple enough to see where the humans had gone. Footmarks were clear in the dusty surface, which seldom suffered significant disturbance – unlike the gas giant hanging above, filling three quarters of the sky, where winds reached almost 400 miles an hour. It looked as if the humans were dragging something, possibly a cart of some sort, because there were shallow ruts accompanying their tracks. Seguidor wondered whether they might be here to collect samples, for some unknown reason. The actions of humanity were frequently unfathomable and always illogical, he knew. They might be looking for some valuable ore, or a scarce resource. But why they'd disappeared from his tracking equipment was a mystery. He was so close, he should easily detect them.

Suddenly both footprints and wheel tracks came to an abrupt halt. Surely the humans did not possess teleport technology? Making an incomplete report to Zoltan with guesses would not be acceptable. He must investigate further. Close inspection of the ground revealed a faint line in the soil. It appeared that something had opened and closed, allowing some soil to trickle into a hole before it was reclosed. The result was a faint indentation. The dead moon of an uninhabitable planet had an artificial entrance. He'd found what he was sent for. Evidence of humanity beyond the settlements already destroyed. But before sharing this information with his master, Seguidor must ensure it wasn't just an abandoned base. That the humans had come here was indisputable, but they might have found nothing.

Seeking an active radio frequency, Seguidor sought a code which would open the portal. It didn't take long. A combination of pulses at differing intervals and pressures produced movement in the ground and the cover to the staircase suddenly drew back, giving him access. As he descended, the entrance closed behind him. His internal lights came on and, unknown to him, his transponder ceased to be in contact with his base.

He reached the metal door without even noticing the passageway lights had come on. It opened for him and he stepped though.

'Your robot set off the alarm,' Leka told us, later that evening. 'You didn't tell me it was armed. But then, I never asked, did I? It destroyed an interloper in the top entrance hall.'

After an increasingly tense few hours, during which nobody spoke to us, I almost didn't notice his choice of "destroyed" rather than killed. What had followed us?

'Our detection system shows no record of another ship approaching, so we sent out a patrol to look at your own vessel. You apparently brought a passenger with you.' He looked accusingly at Evelyn, ignoring me as an irrelevance. The blank expression on her face should have told him it was news to her. And perhaps it did. For he didn't place her under immediate arrest.

'I ... I didn't know ...' she stammered.

'We had the stowaway?' I asked, partly to reassert my significance in our little tableau, but also to introduce the concept of an unknown passenger. If that were needed. Leka turned to look at me.

'There's evidence of a hatch in the engine compartment having been opened. One of my men bravely entered to see if there was anyone – or anything – inside, but it was empty. He did, however, report there was no internal communication with the main part of the ship. Of course, there never is, in Martian shuttles and small craft.' He smiled weakly. He probably recognised Evelyn's – our – innocence, but was worried.

'Come with me,' he ordered.

We were taken to a sophisticated control room, which contained banks of monitors covering many areas of the habitation, as well as some outside views. One of these covered our ship, another, Eddie, now being examined in a laboratory.

'We've watched your ship ever since you arrived. Yes,' he smiled, genuinely this time, 'we saw you land and followed your progress. Once you'd arrived, we continued passive recording. Watch this.' He motioned for a technician to replay images from a few hours earlier. We saw a tall, regularly featured man climb out of a small opening on the side of the craft which we'd never noticed, and make his way slowly towards the camera position. Shortly before he reached it, he clearly discovered and accessed the entrance. After he entered, nothing else was seen.

'The electronic signals we detected when it left the shuttle ceased the moment the hatch closed, as expected, chairman,' said the technician. 'Whoever it was communicating with won't know what happened.' The camera changed to inside the corridor, as the figure approached the metal door and passed through. A third camera then revealed the confrontation between the figure and Albert. 'We've had to slow this down to a thousandth of the actual speed, chairman. It happened so fast.'

'Of course, your robot took only a microsecond to realise it was an android, not a person,' said Leka. 'No spacesuit.' We watched as a minute pulse radiated out from Eddie and the android exploded, rather than crumpling to the ground, as a man would have. 'Just as well we haven't evolved to exist in a vacuum,' he grinned.

Chapter 16 – Planning for survival

'This means the Centaurians know where we are,' said Evelyn, processing the implications of what we'd learned more quickly that I. I'd simply been proud of Eddie's efficiency – and relieved there was no longer any danger. Her words shattered my confidence.

'Yes. We have a problem,' replied Leka briefly. 'Conversely, we know the electronic signals being issued by the android were targeted at an area in space where no spacecraft are detectable within a light month of here. Even if their craft is that close and capable of speeds of up to 10% of the speed of light, we must have years before an invasion can arrive.'

'But what if they are closer, and their signature masked by a larger object. Perhaps the sun, or even Jupiter itself?' suggested Evelyn. As an astrophysicist, she could visualise distances and speeds more easily than most. 'If they are the other side of the sun, which is more likely that near Jupiter, given they couldn't have known where we were headed until after we left Earth, they could get here in much under two years. Whatever their top speed, there shouldn't be time to reach it in such a relatively short this distance.'

Leka briefly considered matters, before calling for Kerensa to join us. She can't have been far away, as she arrived quickly. He outlined our thinking and asked for her view. The longer we got to know him, the clearer it became how he always sought advice from the most qualified person available before making his own decision.

'Based on the available data, which is limited,' she said, after careful deliberation, 'I believe we can assume there's at least twelve months for us to prepare our defences. Lieutenant Commander Starr is probably correct about the Centaurians' having followed her and we can assume this as the worst-case scenario. If we act on it, we'll be prepared whatever happens.'

'If the androids are somewhere near in force,' I added, 'we can expect an attack relatively soon. But what if there's only a token force here. They might feel the need for reinforcements, in which case there could be a delay of years, even decades before they arrive. We might easily be lulled into a false sense of security if nothing happens quickly. That would be dangerous.'

'Mr Adams makes a good point, chairman, but from the little we know of the Centaurians, they attack with relatively small forces and expect their superior technology to carry them through. After all, they need only inflict a limited amount of targeted damage to make a settlement such as this uninhabitable. I assume you have something else in mind?'

Everyone looked at me expectantly, especially Evelyn, who might respect my intellect, but had no reason to look upon me as a military strategist.

'I've had an idea which might help'' I replied. 'We know Eddie was able to destroy the android. It might have been a lucky shot, or simply something the Centaurians were unprepared for. I assume your scientists are currently analysing him to see if you can replicate his weaponry, which I'm sure you can. But is it safe to assume the androids are unaware of what's happened to their representative?

'Yes, I think so,' said Leka. 'Our settlement is very well screened from remote electronic surveillance, largely due to Jupiter's magnetic field. They must know it's missing, but we can surmise information about the android's destruction cannot have escaped from the underground passageway where your robot was so effective.'

'In that case, what's to prevent us from moving away from Ganymede, as if we'd failed to discover our objective, and were looking for another possible base. The putative "mothership" would presumably follow us, rather than wasting time visiting a dead moon.'

Nobody spoke for a long time. The silence extended so long, I feared I'd made a stupid suggestion and nobody wanted to be the first to point out the obvious errors in my logic.

I didn't understand, until later, that everyone was thinking through the implications of my plan. For Evelyn, who would have to pilot her craft into obvious danger, it meant leaving an embryonic friendship with Leka. For Leka, while that consideration also occurred to him, he was calculating how quickly we'd have to leave to make the exit convincing and how many men he would have to send with us, to fight the androids. For Kerensa, the question was how quickly might they replicate our "weapon" and what to do about the lack of future reports from the android to its masters.

Eventually she spoke.

'I see little alternative to your suggestion, Mr Adams. But if you move off now, why should the supposed mothership follow you? Wouldn't they simply sit hidden, waiting to see where you went next before following? And what about the lack of reports from the spy?'

Like a dog with a bone, I was unwilling to abandon my suggestion without some defence.

'Might we somehow analyse its past messages and then create false ones?' I posited.

'It might work, but we have only one brief transmission and no way of knowing what it meant,' said Leka. 'On the other hand, the lack of reports might be the very thing which solves the problem of why they should follow. If they hear nothing more, they'll have to assume either something's gone wrong with the android, or it's been compromised. In either case, they'll surely want to find out which. Intervention might be their only course of action.'

'Assuming they don't simply write off their spy and continue playing a long game. We know they're masters of that,' said Kerensa.

'I think it's a risk worth taking,' Leka concluded. He ended the meeting by sending us back to our quarters with a strict injunction to rest. He'd see us later, he said; although I suspect he was then talking to Evelyn.

'I'm not a clone, am I?' We were sitting together in our shared sitting room, both pretending to read while privately deep in individual thought. I was thinking through the embryonic plan in my mind, Evelyn clearly worrying about what had brought us to the current situation.

'Does it matter? You're still you. But for what it's worth, I don't think so. A clone would be identical in every way to its original, but surely wouldn't share the memories accumulated over a lifetime. Even if the synapses of the brain have been replicated, wouldn't the way they are connected differ? You remember your mother, your childhood and training. Your early lovers,' I added teasingly, thinking of Leka. 'A clone would share your mindset, even ambitions. But I can't believe creating a clone from your DNA could have given you all those memories.'

'But what if the androids have a way of scanning your mind and then imprinting it onto the clone's brain? How would I know if I'm me – or me mark two?'

'If they had such an ability, wouldn't they have put your memories into an android? Their bodies are far more reliable than ours. And if they could scan your brain, why bother with this charade? They could have found everything you know and avoided all this fuss. No. I think you're you.' Evelyn looked relieved. She stood up and walked over to where I was sitting, planting a friendly, dry kiss on my brow.

'Thanks. I needed the reassurance. Now, I'm going to have a shower and put on fresh clothes for the evening.'

'Got a hot date?' I chided, without rancour. She blushed and smiled secretly, but said nothing. Only when I went to bed much later, did I realise I'd not seen her all evening.

My time hadn't been wasted, either. I'd thought about the possible outcomes of several different courses of action. Each had merits and disadvantages and eventually decided to consult Councilwoman Kerensa. She was only too pleased to help and offered to come over and discuss my ideas.

She arrived more promptly than I'd expected and caught me just coming out of the shower, myself. She seemed not the least embarrassed by the sight of a man clad only in his underwear. The showers here not only washed you, but also dried you off. I'd never bothered with such refinements at home. Drying off in the time-honoured fashion of using a bath towel and then throwing it on the floor had always been sufficient for me. And it gave Albert's drones something to do. And him to fuss over. The space shuttle had introduced me to the luxury of hot air blowing me dry after a shower using the finest of sprays under high pressure, to conserve water.

'I didn't know it was *that* sort of party,' she said, displaying an unexpected sense of humour, 'or I wouldn't have brought food.' This was something of an understatement because she was accompanied by a colleague carrying a hamper containing what looked like a banquet, including several forms of alcoholic beverages. Left over from our earlier meal, I wondered?

The woman with her smiled and withdrew, leaving me to wonder what to expect from this encounter. I was not unattracted to the councilwoman, but had no experience of physical relationships and wondered if I might be too old to learn. Besides, Evelyn might come in at any moment. I wouldn't want to embarrass anyone ...

I needn't have worried. Kerensa sat down comfortably on a chair and unpacked the food, motioning for me to go and dress while she did so.

I returned to the sitting room to find her looking at my sketchy notes. She's annotated some and put red lines though others.

'There's nothing particularly wrong with these,' she said, seeing my reaction, 'but I think we should concentrate on the most practical given the limited time available.' She drew one of the scraps of paper towards her, casually asking: 'why do it this way, not on a computer?'

'I felt it safer to put nothing in a format which might be susceptible to interception. If the androids are as sophisticated as we believe, they might access your database – if they now know you're here – and learn what we have in mind. Even sketchy notes on a computer might allow them to extrapolate our plans.'

Kerensa looked at me strangely, then smiled.

'I knew I was right about you,' she said enigmatically. 'OK, let's look at what we have ...'

By the end of a long night, the food was eaten, most of the drinks consumed – and we had the outline of a workable plan.

We would propose to the council a two-pronged approach – with the potential for a third.

As a first step, Evelyn and I would leave quickly and set course for a location which was known not to have a Mars settlement. It was Neptune, another gas giant, but this time out on the edge of the Kuiper belt. So far from Earth, it wasn't known to the ancients who depended entirely on eyesight for their knowledge of the universe, Neptune had

14 satellites, several of which were large enough for underground habitations. Triton, the biggest, was only a little smaller than Earth's moon and followed a retrograde orbit round its planet, each one about a seventh shorter than Ganymede's round Jupiter. We'd have a complement of guards and the weapons Leka was having developed based on Eddie's, which could easily be replicated in time.

Chapter 17 – A new mood

We were in the council chamber again; this time, treated as equals.

I'd outlined the plan Kerensa and I had developed to a rather tired (don't ask) Evelyn over breakfast that morning and she'd accepted it was probably the only thing to do. Now it was time to obtain agreement to the other parts of the strategy.

'The most important thing,' said Drogan who, although not a councillor, was included in our deliberations, 'will be to ensure they follow you.' He knew how vital his role in our scheme would be. The head of security struck me as being remarkably tough for a settlement with no experience of conflict, which filled me with confidence. 'After all, they have no eyes on you anymore. At least as far as we know.'

'Mark has thought of that,' replied Kerensa, ensuring I received credit for my inventiveness. She had long since dropped the "mister". 'Although there hasn't been time for us to learn the code used in what little traffic we intercepted, he suggests we muddle up the last transmission and resend it from the shuttlecraft once it has left Ganymede. It won't make any sense, but it'll alert whatever mother ship there is of the move and – hopefully – imply a communications malfunction. They're bound to seek clarification of the message and we've learned how to intercept it. It can be copied to us here and we'll continue trying to decode it. If we succeed, we can relay a suitable response. If not, we react with gobbledegook. That will keep then interested.'

'I suggest the "gobbledegook" as you put it is ready for instantaneous transmission as soon as a message is received, Kerensa,' said Leka. 'It's highly unlikely there is ever a delay in response from an android, so anything longer than a microsecond might cause suspicion.' It was a good point and I made a note to ensure we have messages prepared. They should be close to the original, to indicate a purely mechanical error.

'I have another suggestion,' said Kerensa. 'I'd like to go on the first craft myself ...' her comment was greeted by a hubbub of amazement from her colleagues, and a wryly suspicious smile from Evelyn. Few had dared leave Ganymede since news of the Maris's destruction had filtered out. For a member of the council to offer to do so was remarkable. And unsettling. Who else might feel obliged to make a similar offer, each asked of him- or herself?

'My reason for this,' she raised her voice over the hubbub, 'is to ensure command of the mission rests where it should, with the elected council of a Mars settlement. Lieutenant Commander Evelyn Starr will captain the ship with an enhanced crew of ten, in addition to myself and Mark Adams. With your agreement, I will command the entire mission and Mark will be my deputy. It is, after all, his plan we'll be following.' I was amazed there was no adverse reaction to this from anyone. Not even Evelyn or Drogan, either of whom might have expected the leadership role. Perhaps they'd been pre-briefed.

'Security chief Drogan will lead a second craft which will leave a week later. The Majestic is larger and can carry a crew of a hundred or more of his operatives. It's faster than the shuttle, which is just as well, because it needs to reach the Kuiper belt first and by a more circuitous route, to avoid detection. His mission will be to join us in an ambush. While the androids attack the shuttlecraft, he will attack them.'

None of the councillors had questioned the existence of the Majestic. It was well known amongst the elite that a vessel had been kept in readiness for millennia. Just in case. But there was an obvious flaw in this and Evelyn asked the inevitable question. 'Won't its launch automatically generate suspicion? This is supposed to be a dead moon. A second spaceship leaving here would prove the habitation exists – the very thing we are trying to avoid having known.'

'We're now relatively certain the Centaurian mothership is somewhere the other side of the sun,' said Magdor, the councilman responsible for telecommunications. 'Launching from the Jupiter side of the moon will mask the point of origin, and a trajectory which leaves planetary orbit on the night side will mask the craft until it is well out of the way. Thereafter, it will rely on simply not being noticed. But in a large cosmos, it's a fair hope.'

Drogan, who was clearly already up to speed, chipped in. 'We'll follow a flight plan which always keeps Jupiter between us and the sun. If the shuttle goes directly towards the Kuiper belt, we've calculated the Centaurians will go in a straight line behind them. We'll be invisible until we're able to lose ourselves in the stellar debris which make it up. It's massively thick and surprisingly dense, given its breadth. I'm confident my party can remain undiscovered, while the androids focus their attention on Kerensa, Mark and Evelyn.' It was the first time he'd referred to us by name.

'There's something else,' added Leka. 'Only a small number of people know this, but we have the approximate co-ordinates of another settlement. It's not technically a settlement at all. It's a massive space station, a hundred times the size of the old Maris. It was sent out as one of the last missions from Mars and got no further than the Kuiper belt before its master decided he'd found an ideal place to settle in peace. The radiation there is sufficient to mask their presence. Unless anything's gone wrong, they've been sitting there for fifteen thousand years. Its population must be upwards of two million by now. Part of Drogan's mission is to contact them and seek support before the ambush. We guess they must have more spacecraft than us. And probably armaments. They are, after all, more of a frontier world than us. We're hoping they'll join us in destroying the Centaurian vessel.'

Everyone silently hoped he was correct on all counts.

'That raises the issue of weapons. And training, for that matter,' said another councilwoman. 'How is that progressing?'

'Based on the Earth robot ... Eddie,' Drogan almost stumbled over naming a machine in his response, 'we've been able to replicate hand held versions of the weapon it carries, as well as some significantly larger ones, using similar technology. The downside of these is that they must be operated by people; we don't have the time to create sufficiently intelligent machinery to operate against the androids. Some of these are ground-based, others capable of operating in the air or even in space. Training for this will take time, but so will the journey to our hunting ground. We'll be using flight simulators to acclimatise our men and women to the task.'

'Will this be adequate?' asked Magdor. 'Surely the real experience will be vastly different from interacting with a computer?'

'I've thought of that,' replied Drogan. 'It might sound harsh, but the simulators will give electric shock feedback. It won't be fatal, of course, but it'll make the operators more careful when the time comes. It could save lives.'

'In any case,' added Leka quickly, to prevent criticism of the plan, 'the androids probably won't have battle experience either.' We all knew that was an academic point. They were still machines.

It had been a lengthy meeting and I, for one, was hungry. Evelyn and I found ourselves alone, as everyone else rushed off to execute their part of the plan. For us, a rapid departure left little time for anything more, so we went to find some food.

'So, your girlfriend's coming with us. I'm jealous,' said Evelyn, without rancour. 'Pity I can't bring Leka along.' Her tacit acceptance I must be aware of her burgeoning relationship with the chairman took something off any potential embarrassment. But I had to set her straight.

'Kerensa's not my "girlfriend", although I admit admiring her.' You know there's no room in my heart for anyone but you.' I said the words with a smile, but she didn't return it. Perhaps I'd overstepped the mark, but it was too late to retract. Anyway, I do feel strongly protective towards her; but in a fraternal way. 'Of course, there's no chance of Leka accompanying Drogan, I suppose? At least that way, he'd be in at the kill. And you'd get to see him again.' This time I was rewarded with a warm smile. And a sisterly punch on the arm. At least I hope it was sisterly; I wouldn't want to be on the receiving end of that fist with any weight behind it.

'No. His duty is here,' she replied wistfully. 'Perhaps, when this is all over ...' If only.

As we ate lunch, we were approached by a tall young officer. His bushy fair hair made him look about forty, but given his rank insignia, he must have been older.

'I'm Captain Pakeman. I've been assigned to lead the troops on your shuttle, so I thought I'd introduce myself.' It was an army rank which made him junior to Evelyn's space navy one.

'Take a seat, captain,' said Evelyn. 'Welcome to the party. We're going to be in close confines for a long time, so we should get to know each other. Have you eaten?'

As we continued our meal, Pakeman told us a little about himself and his team. They were already a unit and had undertaken limited combat training. Ten percent of each generation had to undergo military service, selected by lottery, and a number of these opted to stay on as a career, at the end of basic training. Like all soldiers, they were keen on keeping the peace, but couldn't wait to see some action. Initial weapons instruction was progressing well. His men – there were no women in his command, which was unusual – would only be using hand-held weapons. Their role would be as shock troops and, he freely admitted, was to be expendable. Their primary order, was to keep the three principals – as he termed Kerensa, Evelyn and me – safe, while attacking whatever objective he was ordered to.

As commander of the vessel, Evelyn wanted to know a little about the men who would be temporarily under her command, so Pakeman filled her in. He knew and liked them all, which augured well for the mission. They would fight cohesively.

'Do we have to keep referring to the shuttlecraft in such an abstract way?' he asked, as we separated to complete our personal preparations. 'It seems so impersonal and I know the men would be happier to have something more "individual" on the side of the craft they'll serve – and may die – in.'

'Have you any suggestions, captain?' asked its commander.

He thought for a moment, not expecting to have been asked for an opinion. 'How about Endeavour? It was the name given to one of the first space shuttles on Earth. I remember reading about it at school. It was retired, honourably early in the Atomic Era. Perhaps we might be as fortunate.'

Chapter 18 – Departure

The small troop under Captain Pakeman's command was put into stasis before Endeavour lifted off from Ganymede, to mask their life-signs. The presence of Kerensa and the captain also had to be screened, but in their case a bio-suppressor attached to their wrists gave off a signal disguising their presence with random electrical signals. There was no need to do so for Evelyn and me, of course; the androids already knew about us. Sometime during the year-long flight, there'd be advanced weapons and tactical training for the soldiers, who would then be "screened", too. The first half of the trip would therefore include planning and weapons familiarisation for the leaders, while the second half would be devoted to bringing the troop up to speed.

Simultaneously with the launch, Eddie sent the fake message to the mothership, hopefully convincing them he was the android with now faulty communications equipment.

'We can't know whether this will work,' admitted Kerensa, 'but at least we tried. And there's nothing to tell the Centaurians Ganymede is anything more than a lifeless moon. Set course for the Kuiper belt, please, Evelyn.'

'Already laid in, Commander. We'll head for Saturn and swing round it to get some momentum before heading towards the belt. We're using the crypto-planet Pluto, as our rendezvous because it's easily identifiable.' We'd decided Neptune might be a step too far, given the protection which the Kuiper belt would afford for an ambush.

'I'll check on my men and the equipment now,' said Pakeman, as soon as they were in transit. He looked in on the stasis pods to ensure everyone had survived the launch, before going to the large bay at the rear of the craft for weapons practice. He'd need to be totally proficient in their use and care if he was to lead his troop professionally. He spent several days stripping down every item to its base components and then reassembling them. Eddie became his constant companion. Guiding him when he faltered with the unfamiliar technology and helping him practice aiming and firing in a simulated environment. Live fire was completely impossible, not simply because of potential damage to the craft, but also because this might be detected – and more importantly, analysed – by the Centaurians.

Initially no more comfortable with personifying machines than had been Drogan, Pakeman quickly became to rely on his new companion in an unexpected way. Eddie became his sergeant in all but name. providing advice, support and guidance whenever needed. But unobtrusively so. I suppose, I ignored Eddie in the same way as I had Albert, at home. He was a constant factor, but one to which no attention needed to be paid. For Pakeman, he was a valuable aide.

Gradually, Eddie took on responsibility for monitoring the stasis pods, as well as his irregular communications to the mother ship.

'I hope this isn't too frequent,' commented Evelyn after one transmission. 'We don't know how often the android reported. Or if it was only when the mother ship contacted him. I'm trying to tie them in to a course correction which is significant enough to be noticed, to explain the contact.'

'I wouldn't worry too much,' Kerensa told her. 'According to Magdor, before we left, the android would have been sending constant telemetry, before it was destroyed. This should explain its absence.'

'Seguidor is transmitting nonsense,' Zoltan told his deputy. Hierarchy amongst the androids of Alpha Centauri was as structured as it had been on Earth, prior to their departure on the four-light-year journey to create the base for a humanity which never followed. There was no logical reason for it; rather it was a learned structure which had never been abandoned as the artificial intelligence of the original robots became increasingly self-aware and then fully sentient. They were, to all intents and purposes, a new life-form, albeit without the one essential requirement of being capable of self-reproduction. They got around that by creating new androids artificially.

'What do you wish us to do?' Naibu knew better than to make decisions on his own account. His predecessor had tried to do so and found himself reassigned on a benighted mission; following some woman in the hope of destroying what remained of humanity. If he was honest, Naibu couldn't understand the need for such wanton destruction of those who had given life to his race. He wondered whether it was fear, or envy, which drove Admiral Zoltan in his quest. As androids increasingly faced the same challenges as humanity, it seemed to him they were becoming more alike, rather than diverging in development.

But his was not to question orders, simply to obey them.

'Former Commander Seguidor is clearly faulty, commander. The humans cannot know we are monitoring them, so we will follow them at a distance and see what they are doing. Their visit to Jupiter III seems to have been abortive, as they were only there for three days. Perhaps they are leading us to another potential habitation. I never believed the woman didn't know where to find her kind. Releasing her, even against the orders of the Supreme Council, was the right choice.

'The Centaurian ship is moving from behind the sun.' Evelyn had been monitoring their likely position for indications of activity ever since their departure from Ganymede. After a week, she was beginning to wonder whether they had it wrong; that the android Eddie had destroyed was unsupported. Now their suspicions were vindicated. 'My God!' she exclaimed. 'It's massive. The readings it's giving off are far larger than anything we ever built. At least five to ten times the volume of the Last Hope, from what Leka told us.' We were sitting alone on the bridge, although her exclamation was bound to have attracted the others.

'Last Hope?' I'd not previously heard the expression.

'The name given to the space station Leka mentioned – the last one to leave Mars. Kerensa told me it was called that before news of Maris's destruction reached Mars. Ironic, really, because that's what it's become: *our* last hope. If they won't help us destroy the android vessel, what chance does humanity have of surviving?'

'Can we warn Ganymede and the Majestic they're on their way?'

'No,' commanded Kerensa, who had just arrived. 'Communication of any sort would risk giving away our knowledge of their pursuit, as well as Majestic's existence, if not location. And the fact that there's someone on Ganymede to receive a message. I'm sure they're making the same observations as us. We can't contact them. We just have to hope Drogan and the others meet us as agreed.' And manage to locate the Last Hope first, we all added silently.

'It seems Councilwoman Kerensa's assessment of Mark Adams was correct,' Drogan told his military chief, Lieutenant Colonel Wogon. The Majestic had departed as planned and was on course for the putative location of the Last Hope, with the aim of seeking assistance in fighting the androids. 'He read the situation correctly. A massive vessel had just emerged from behind the sun. It must be large enough to hold hundreds of thousands of androids.'

Wogon was unusual for a Ganymede soldier. Rougher than Captain Pakeman, he'd achieved his rank through hard work and driving his men aggressively in training and what little conflict occurred on a relatively small settlement. Drogan has always resented the independence afforded to the army. It should, he believed, have been part of his security fiefdom, given there were no external threats of which anyone had been aware for millennia. Yet the founding fathers of the settlement had insisted on separation of the forces. And there had been occasions, during the rare internecine fighting between colonies, when this had proved a good idea. But that was long ago.

'Nothing will enable us to destroy so many, unaided,' said Wogon. He was eager for a fight, but not suicidal. He would look for allies and a strategy which would allow the best opportunity to inflict maximum damage on the enemy – while offering a chance of survival. 'Let's find the Last Hope quickly.'

'We know roughly where it must be. We can't send a message, but we can start looking for signs of unusual radiation as soon as we reach the Kuiper belt. It's less dense than the Asteroid belt, so we have a chance of detecting something.'

'Well, as far as we know, the androids have never managed to detect them ...' offered Wogon.

'No, but they had less incentive – and no precise knowledge of what they were looking for. We do.'

'What's going on lieutenant?' It seemed an innocent enough question from the man in charge of the Last Hope. But with Admiral Petersen, it was best to be precise and factual. No more, no less.

'Sir! You will recall a report some time ago of two vessels passing through the belt on their way towards the sun?' Even if the admiral didn't, it was best to assume otherwise, Craven decided. 'The smaller craft visited Mars, then Earth, before heading for Jupiter. There may still be a settlement on Ganymede, it's third moon, although we don't know if it's already fallen to the Centaurians. Nothing's been heard for a long time.'

'Yes, yes, I know all that. Get on with it lieutenant,' said the senior officer impatiently, leaving his junior uncertain how much the old man did remember.

'Well the smaller ship has left Ganymede heading out of the solar system and the large android ship has just left its station behind the sun and started what appears to be pursuit, sir.'

'How should that concern us, lieutenant? Unless they pass within an astronomical unit, there's no way they'll notice us.' He thought for a moment. He didn't want to be the commander of the Last Hope responsible for its loss. Not that anyone would know. When settlements were destroyed by the androids, there were no survivors. None. But that wasn't the point. It was a matter of pride to protect his massive vessel. And almost a million lives on aboard. Only a small percentage of them were military, of course. Most simply lived out their lives peacefully as had countless generations before them. But as Admiral, it was his responsibility to protect them. And he must.

He continued in an even voice, although he had a deep foreboding. 'Continue to monitor both vessels, lieutenant. And watch out for any other anomalies. Not just from within the solar system, but beyond it. The Centaurians come from four light years away. For all we know this might be the start of an invasion of the home planets. God knows why they should bother, but best to be prepared.' He left the observation room in which he'd been talking with the junior officer and went for a walk round his command centre. Thinking.

Chapter 19 – Training

For six months, Captain Pakeman spent four-hours a day familiarising himself with the new weapons his men would use in the forthcoming fight with the androids. Notwithstanding the success against an unprepared Centaurian on Ganymede scored by the robot Eddie, there was no knowing how effective the scientists' rushed development the scientists would be. Pakeman therefore devoted hours to considering how they might be brought to bear in various circumstances.

Actual use would depend on whether for offence or defence; for boarding an enemy vessel, or repelling an incursion onto the Endeavour. Or even the Majestic, if they managed to team up with Colonel Wogon. He'd served under the man before and knew him to be brave and resourceful. But he was also harsh on his men and could often be gung-ho. It would be for Pakeman to ensure the safety of the men under his command in a fight. This meant concentrating on the minutiae of their preparation. Similar measures would be in hand on the larger vessel, although it would be equipped with larger weaponry, including some self-propelled versions.

Once satisfied with his preparations, Pakeman invited Evelyn and me to try out the simulations he'd prepared for the platoon.

'Put on the headsets and take hold of one of the guns,' he ordered. 'Don't worry, they're not real, but the weight and operation are identical to the real thing. Your robot helped me design them and the programme you're about to encounter. The ship's computer built the virtual reality environment to its specification.

My head enclosed, I found myself in a strange world, looking around the vast space of a hangar, as if we had just disembarked from the shuttlecraft inside the enemy ship.

Next to me, Evelyn wore a spacesuit and held a gun. I looked down and saw I was similarly clad – which explained the digital heads-up display I could see on the visor in front of me. Pakeman's voice sounded metallically in the earpiece.

'This simulation is for an attack on the enemy vessel. It assumes no atmosphere, as androids don't need one. I have versions for conditions with air, weightlessness and darkness, too. I've had to guess aspects of their ship's layout, so the simulation changes automatically between each exercise. That way, I can train people to react to what they encounter, rather than what they remember. Let's give it a go.'

The simulation jumped, and Evelyn and I were suddenly walking away from Endeavour, Pakeman behind us.

'I'll be on the first few missions to guide you. Later you'll be on your own. The men won't, but you need greater independence of action, in case you have to assume tactical command.' No need to explain why.

My eyes shifted to the right, reacting to a movement behind a packing case. Turning, I saw a tall person, like the android Eddie had destroyed. Without thinking, I aimed roughly and engaged the trigger. Its head dissolved into nothing.

'Very good. You'll see targeting is automatic. Look at what you want to hit, and the weapon will do the rest. When fighting in an atmosphere, you'll be wearing a visor for the heads-up display and communications. Otherwise, the spacesuit fulfils the function. Let's move on.'

We walked towards what looked like an exit without further incident, but as we reached it, another person appeared in view. A slightly taller figure, but much more thickly set. It had a menacing look on its face. Evelyn saw him first and fired, as I had. This time, it didn't explode but crumpled to the ground.

Pakeman laughed. 'Well done commander. You've just shot Colonel Wogon. He's Drogan's number two and will lead the assault forces. In this simulation, they'd landed ahead of us and secured the hangar, although they'd clearly missed the android Mark shot.' He must have noticed her crestfallen appearance and sagging gun arm. 'Don't worry, he's a brute; I can think of a dozen soldiers who'd like to take the shot! That's why he's in the simulation. It'll give them something to laugh about, and remind them of the importance of identifying the target before they fire. Let's move on.'

We progressed through a variety of passages and rooms, destroying androids as we went whilst trying to avoid killing our colleagues. There was a fine line between delaying long enough to tell friend from foe and getting shot while we hesitated. Each of us "died" several times after taking too long to identify the target correctly before firing.

'I am monitoring your progress.' Eddie's voice came over our earpieces. 'I do not think you can outshoot the androids like this. They'll fire on sight. Their brains work faster than yours and they can accept accidentally destroying a few of their own. With your permission, I believe we should modify the weapons to make it impossible for them to harm humans, captain. That way, you won't lose vital microseconds evaluating your target.'

The captain's avatar looked at Evelyn. She was, after all the ranking officer present. She nodded as much as the spacesuit allowed – it was unbelievably realistic.

'That seems a sensible suggestion, Eddie. Make it so,' she ordered. The change within the simulation was instantaneous and we quickly found it possible to take out all the androids we were faced with. In fact, we seemed to be unrealistically successful. After half an hour, there were none left. We were in control of the enemy ship.

'Captain, is it possible we will be able to dispose of the enemy so easily? Surely, we must expect to suffer some casualties?' I asked.

'Sorry Mark, I should have explained there are five levels of difficulty within the simulation. This was level one, to allow you to familiarise yourself with the process. Councilwoman Kerensa says nobody will be able to go on a mission unless they reach level five and "live". It's a matter of mission success, as well as individual survival. Unless sufficient people reach the required level of proficiency – and that means virtually all of us – we can't proceed.'

By the time we were half way to our objective, we were ready to revive Pakeman's troop and start their training. They would fight under his command when away from the ship, but Evelyn and I would accompany them as unofficial lieutenants, able to take command should he fall. We both fervently hoped he wouldn't as we could scarcely afford to lose his tactical expertise.

Drogan's troops on the Majestic were into their training long before those of us on the Endeavour. It was a larger force and had more to do. Especially those who would pilot the tiny spaceships – also capable of flying within an atmosphere – which would provide what heavy firepower we possessed. There were only sixteen of them, in four wings, but they were fleet and capable. As were the specially selected pilots.

The latter were chosen not for their military prowess, but for sporting ability. One of the most popular – and competitive – pastimes on Ganymede was zero-gravity polo. A large arena had been set aside outside the artificial gravity system used to combat the moon's weak pull throughout the habitation. Lightweight scooters were used to pursue a target ball within a double-cube of airspace, with the aim of knocking it through the opponent's undefended goal. Teams of five were set against each other, much of the skill involving manoeuvring the craft into a position in which they could be used to nudge the ball. It required considerable dexterity and Leka, a long-term fan of the game, had decided its proponents would be ideal for the task in hand. Those selected were wildly excited with the prospect of participating in something so important and challenging. Whether their enthusiasm would survive combat – or even just serving under Wogon – was something only time would tell.

The Majestic was a faster craft than ours, so reached the region of space where the Last Hope was thought to be, well ahead of us.

'Surely we can send them a message now?' Wogon complained to Drogan. He was irked by the need to seek permission for anything, especially from the security chief. Yet he respected the chain of command – when it was unavoidable. 'They must be aware of our approach anyway, and we don't know precisely where they are.'

'Patience, colonel,' replied the security chief. 'We have a good idea of their general position and our equipment should find them without assistance. They are undoubtedly, as you say, monitoring us. The Centaurians and Kerensa's team, too, I'd imagine. If I were them, I'd be highly suspicious. Not to mention livid, should we do anything to give away their location …'

He was interrupted by a junior officer.

'Commander, we have positively identified the Last Hope. Its signature is incredibly weak, they're so well masked. Had we not known where to look, we'd never have found them. They are close to a group of large objects, each obscuring them from a different direction. Goodness knows how they don't collide, sir.'

'I suspect that's thanks to tractor beams, Lieutenant Brody. Those objects have probably kept the station concealed ever since it arrived. Make a course to fly past the group, then squeeze us into the space between the asteroids, alongside them.'

'Shall I deploy the decoy, commander?'

'At the very last minute, Brody. It must look to the Centaurians – if they're watching – as if we are simply making a minor course correction. The Last Hope will see the manoeuvre and recognise we're disguising their location.'

The Majestic couldn't afford to slow down, for risk of the manoeuvre being noticed by the androids. So, as it passed the cluster of asteroids and the decoy was released to continue their course out of the solar system, the pilot quickly turned to orbit the gravitational field created by the massive space station and its protectors, slowing gradually. Simultaneously, the ship went 'dark' – all electrical equipment being reduced to a minimum to avoid detection.

A single, tiny light blinked out of the darkness at the centre of the cluster of asteroids.

Chapter 20 – Coming together

Admiral Petersen, aboard the Last Hope, had long wondered why the androids hadn't invaded the home solar system. It wasn't so much a strategic objective as a symbolic one. To have the two home worlds under 'alien' control would have been demoralising to any remaining Martian outposts. Not that anyone knew for certain whether there were any. If the Centaurians were confident they'd destroyed everyone – except the Last Hope, of course – there'd be no point in such a gesture. It could have no significance for mere machines, could it?

But what were the approaching ships? Perhaps they contained survivors of some sort of internecine conflict, looking for salvation within the solar system. Well, their trip was wasted. Generations of admirals had monitored Earth and Mars for any signs of animation; the start of some sort of initiative to reach out to those who'd left, so long ago. His forerunners had decided there was practically nobody on Earth or Mars and discounted it as a source of aid. That said, it was ages since any evidence of conflict had indicated ongoing conflict between androids and their creators. If there were any habitations left, they must be as well concealed as the Last Hope.

Now, someone was trying to find them, to disturb the long, uneasy tranquillity. Damn them. And they'd brought company.

His silent reverie was disturbed by the lieutenant.

'What is it, Craven?'

'The larger of the two Martian vessels has entered our defensive shield, sir. It sent a probe to continue its original trajectory and has gone dark. But we can track its position, as it's so close. What are your orders, admiral?'

Petersen thought for a few moments before answering. This craft threatened his desire to remain hidden, but destroying it would draw attention. The pursuing space station must be aware of the visiting craft, so an explosion would require investigation. Which would bring them too close.

'Where's the shuttle craft, lieutenant?'

'Still a considerable way off, sir. It's heading in the general direction of Pluto.'

'Very well. Send a signal to the orbiting craft. And Craven? Do it discreetly.'

The young lieutenant saluted with a sharp 'aye-aye, sir', the nautical double affirmative had been used since time immemorial. He returned to his post, wondering how best to communicate without risking detection. A directed signal should be safe, but one never knew. Given the speed at which the target vessel was travelling, it was always possible the tight beam might miss and go off into space, where it would be susceptible to interception. There was, however, an alternative. Every cadet since time immemorial had had to learn an old Earth language called Morse. Who these "Morse" were, was lost in the mist of time. The race must have died out before the Atomic Era. But the benefit of their language was that it consisted entirely of dots and dashes which could be sent by a variety of means. Using a light, pointed at one of the asteroids, would make it less likely to spill out of their protective cocoon and be intercepted. The orbiting craft wouldn't see it all the time, of course. But they would eventually intersect the beam and be able to read the message.

Entering a cabin with a porthole, Craven darkened the ambient light before uncovering the opening and using a hand lamp to send his signal.

Dot, dot. Dash, dot, dot. Dot. Dash, dot. Dash. Dot, dot. Dot, dot, dash, dot. Dash, dot, dash, dash. Dash, dot, dash, dash. Dash, dash, dash. Dot, dot, dash. Dot, dash, dot. Dot, dot, dot. Dot. Dot, dash, dash, dash. Dot, dot, dash, dot. 'IDENTIFY YOURSELF'. The hand lamp recorded the sequence and repeated it, while he held it to the window, watching for a reply. He stood there for hours.

Security Chief, and part time Commander, Drogan had retired to his cabin to consider why there had been no reaction from the Last Hope. Was it possible there was nobody there? It was dark, but it would be if it wanted to avoid detection. Would it be safe to send one of his small fighters to investigate? It would be good practice for them in space, as opposed to using the simulators.

'Commander Drogan to the bridge, please.' Brody's voice sounded over the ship's communicator.

At last, something was happening. Let's hope it's good news, he thought as he moved swiftly to the command post.

'They're signalling, sir,' reported Brody, his excitement brightening his eyes as little had for a long time. 'It's a code we all learned as cadets. They're asking who we are. Shall I reply?'

Drogan considered for a moment. It might be a trap; the Centaurians might already be in possession of the space station. If so they were doomed. But better safe than sorry.

'Send a message exactly as follows, Brody. "MAJESTIC OUT OF ZEUS III REQUESTING OLYMPIAN WELCOME." Just that. If they're human, they'll work it out. If not, they at least probably won't be able to tell where we've come from.' *Before they destroy us.*

The bewildered junior officer went to a suitable porthole and flickered the message to the Last Hope. He had to send it for half an hour before he saw an acknowledging "OK", sent back. He then watched for at least the same time again until a return message simply stated: "HERA AWAITS."

Drogan smiled, relief and laughter mixed on his craggy face. 'They're human, all right, Brody, and they're inviting us into their docking. I imagine that hasn't been used for a long time.'

'I don't understand, commander. Who is Hera?'

'In Greek mythology, Hera was Zeus's wife. Zeus was the name that ancient people gave to Jupiter, so it was obvious to anyone who knew our history we must be from Ganymede – Jupiter's third moon. The Olympian welcome is a rather crude way of allowing us full entry rights!'

Drogan called May, the lieutenant commander in charge of navigation, ordering her to set a course for the space station and dock. The approach took several hours, as they were still moving rapidly. Eventually, they saw the aperture through which they must fly, to enter the base. It was smaller than expected, but they were guided by a tractor beam, which disabled their own controls and brought them safely inside.

'That's not a manoeuvre we've performed recently,' Admiral Petersen told Drogan when they met. It was a massive understatement, as both men knew. 'We've been monitoring the ship following you and it looks as if they've bought your deception. They're watching your decoy. Which is just as well for all of us.' This was the first confirmation Drogan had that they had, after all, been monitored.

'Thanks for having us aboard, Admiral. I'm glad we seem not to have given away your position. You must be aware there's another, smaller vessel behind us. That's one of ours.'

'Yes, we know. Is it another decoy?'

'No, Admiral. It contains some of our people who have been followed from Earth. We need your help to destroy the Centaurian space station behind them – and us, apparently. They'll lead the attack, but we'll join them with reinforcements at a point in space near where Pluto will be in four weeks' time. But we can't do it alone.'

'Tell me more Commander Drogan.'

'We can assume the Majestic has established contact,' Evelyn told us. 'The signal shot past where we think the Last Hope is two days ago. If they'd failed, I suspect we would have seen some other activity.'

We were sitting in the control cabin, which doubled as a conference area. Kerensa, Pakeman, Evelyn and I were now satisfied with the men's training – not to mention our own – and impatient to start the next phase of our self-imposed mission.

'The main problem is that we have only a limited idea what the inside of the android spacecraft looks like,' said the captain. 'I can't plan an attack without specific information. And as for co-ordinating our activities with Colonel Wogon and his team … well, there's little chance of that. We'll all be operating blind.' It was a discussion we'd had many times before and always come to the same conclusion. There was no answer.

'Forgive me for interrupting.' Eddie was such a part of our everyday life, we tended not to notice his presence. And it was unusual for him to initiate comment, so this must be important. 'We might have access to information about their vessel, if the assumption Commander Starr and this shuttle were held on it by the androids is correct.' Everyone looked at him in amazement. Was he suggesting the ship would somehow be able to remember its time aboard the space station?

'Can you explain?' I asked, careful not to sound dismissive. Over many years of dealing with Albert, I'd noticed he was susceptible to sulking if he felt he was being ignored or made fun of. I assumed such a trait might have been transferred to his mobile progeny.

'Of course, sir. I regret not having calculated the possibility sooner, but it occurred to me that the androids might have installed software into this vessel which enabled their observer to monitor its movements undetected. By identifying – and reverse engineering – this, we might be able to get a sense of what the mother ship is like and how it operates.'

Evelyn, who was first and foremost a scientist looked wonderingly at the robot for several minutes, during which nobody spoke. Eddie was, as usual, motionless under scrutiny.

'That's a stroke of genius, Eddie,' she said warmly. 'Have you searched for it yet?

'No, commander. I have done nothing yet in case you disapproved. But I can start work immediately.'

'Is there any danger of them being able to detect our attempt?' I asked. 'If so, it might give away our plan to attack them. They can't possibly anticipate what we have in mind. It would be suicide ...' We stared at each other for a moment. It was the first time any of us had verbalised the hopelessness of our mission.

'I believe we can isolate the computer from external monitoring, Mr Adams. Of course, there is no guarantee we will be able to find the information the captain needs for his assault, but it is worth the attempt. With your permission, I will commence immediately.'

Within a week – two weeks out from our planned rendezvous with the Majestic – Eddie reported greater success than we had imagined possible.

'Not only have I been able to decode their communications protocols, but I have sufficient information from the limited database they downloaded to the Endeavour, to identify possible points of entry to their vessel. And some potential weak points. Apparently, the

Endeavour was programmed to return to them under certain circumstances.'

'What are those?' asked Evelyn, who had the greatest interest, since she was putatively the vessel's sole occupant.

'If there are no life-signs within a kilometre of the sensors in the engine compartment, commander.'

Chapter 21 – Reaching out

'This is foolishness, Admiral Petersen, and you know it.' Few people could talk plainly to the head of the Last Hope, but General Stuart was one of them. Mrs Petersen was the other – not to mention his daughter, a self-willed woman of less than fifty, whom he would dearly like to marry off, if he could only find someone suitable. Perhaps Craven …?

The two senior officers were discussing Drogan's request for assistance on behalf of Ganymede in strict privacy. If they acquiesced, everyone would learn soon enough. Otherwise, it was best if nobody knew they'd abandoned one of the few other remaining Mars settlements. And one of the oldest. It was for this reason that the Majestic's crew had been held incommunicado on their ship and only Drogan and Wogon allowed on the Last Hope. A story had been put about that an unmanned ship had been found drifting and towed alongside, to prevent discovery of their location. How many residents believed this was difficult to tell.

'I'm aware of your views, general. But the fact remains, the android ship is within the solar system and may already be aware of our existence. You and I know full well, no outpost of the Martian diaspora has ever successfully resisted their attack. Striking first may be our sole defence. I believe we have no alternative but to assist our friends.'

'Possibly, but what form should that take? Providing supplies and sending them on their way is theoretically possible, but it risks revealing our precise location to an implacable enemy. We're not certain whether the small shuttlecraft knows where we are, but since they aren't here it's likely not. We could simply destroy this ship and all aboard it, to remain completely hidden. I don't think letting the Majestic leave is realistic. If they're captured in their quixotic attempt to destroy the Centaurian ship, they are bound to betray us; may already have done so simply by visiting.'

'We could refuse assistance but hold the people prisoner, general? I couldn't countenance killing our own. These are all descendants of Mars settlers. Like us.'

'Allowing them to attack the androids is little better than executing them ourselves, admiral. They will be destroyed. It's simply a matter of when … and whether they take us with them.'

The admiral could see the merits of the military commander's argument. But this was a momentous decision and the Ganymede leader had a right to plead his case. He ordered Drogan to be brought to them, alone and in secret.

'Commander, you must understand our position,' the admiral was moving towards Stuart's position, that giving any assistance would be too dangerous. 'Any aid we provide risks our discovery. We've so far escaped, but when the Centaurians discover you sent them after a decoy, they are bound to come back looking for you – and finding us.'

'We're not at all sure they know of our own existence, admiral,' Drogan obfuscated. 'The decoy was insurance in case we'd been spotted. As far as we are aware, they're following the Endeavour, not us. That they haven't deviated from their original course suggests they are still aware only of the single craft. And they knew of that already, given it'd been in their sights for millennia. We're offering you the chance to strike a first successful blow against the race which has destroyed so many of our people. Failure on our part,' he deliberately made it a collective responsibility, 'would simply delay the androids' inevitable victory …'

'… as failure to wipe their vessel out would lead to our annihilation so much sooner. We risk drawing them down on us like avenging demons, if just one of them survives.' The general was clearly against assisting.

Drogan wondered why a military man would want so much to avoid a fight. All soldiers would rather keep the peace. But there comes a time when everyone knows war becomes inevitable. Could it be cowardice, or might there be more sinister motives? They stared at each other, wondering who would, metaphorically, blink first.

It was Admiral Petersen who interrupted the deepening silence between the other two.

'I understand your reticence, General Stuart. But I'm now determined that we should help the commander in his efforts to destroy the Centaurian ship. I insist, however, that this is done in such a way that our precise location – even our existence – cannot be identified. I leave you to work out the details.'

Time had little meaning for the androids, they performed their routine duties and obeyed orders. At least, most of them did. Some were imbued with a level of self-awareness which went beyond artificial intelligence and bordered on imagination. One such was Naibu, deputy commander of the Centaurian starship. He found the effort spent following the small shuttlecraft his admiral had insisted on capturing – and then, many centuries later, releasing – to be disquieting. There had never been any orders to this effect and he increasingly wondered whether Zoltan was not acting beyond his remit. If he tried to ask questions, he was simply told these were matters to which he was not party. Zoltan was, after all, a member of the Supreme Council. Albeit one who had not attended meetings on Centaur for millennia. Was it possible he was acting entirely on his own in this matter? And, if so, what else might he be ignoring orders about? No communications ever came to the ship except through Zoltan, so if they were acting beyond their orders, how could Naibu know?

His musings had reached the stage where he was no longer convinced destroying humanity was either necessary, or even in the best interests of the androids themselves. The original concept of expunging them had been driven partly by a desire for revenge at their abandonment, and partly out of fear for their greater intuitive abilities which would make them a threat to a race with computer brains. They would be unpredictable in a fight.

Was Zoltan right, relentlessly to pursue an edict which might no longer be in force, or even essential? Naibu found himself watching his admiral carefully.

'Commander,' his rapid, if now somewhat circular, reasoning was interrupted by Treban, his immediate deputy. 'There has been a change in the shuttlecraft's trajectory. It is slowing in the proximity of a small planetoid near the Kuiper belt. I believe it is called Pluto. Should we match our speed to theirs?'

'I assume there is still no coherent message from Seguidor, lieutenant commander?'

'No, sir, his transmissions remain unintelligible. In fact, I recommend we ignore him completely now.' Naibu, who had already done so in his mind, agreed.

'We can assume they remain unaware of our pursuit. Nothing suggests they have yet established contact with any settlements. Jupiter III was clearly a dead satellite; perhaps they think one of their settlements might be here, instead. I will recommend to the admiral that we continue with this trajectory at a reduced speed. We may need to alter course later.'

✄

'We've almost reached Pluto, Kerensa. Shall we enter orbit?' During the week since Eddie's discovery of the partial schematic of the Centaurian ship, Evelyn, Pakeman and I had been refining our tactics. We'd devised scenarios involving just us and for ourselves plus the Majestic. We even had one using an additional ship, in case Drogan was successful in securing support from the Last Hope. Details of the enemy vessel had been built into the practice simulations and our platoon trained to within an inch of their lives in how to move stealthily and effectively amongst its myriad rooms and corridors.

'Yes, Evelyn, let's do so. At the very least, the Centaurians will wonder what we're up to.'

'I don't think they know we're onto them, yet. Otherwise they'd have attacked,' I said, agreeing that being unpredictable might give us an edge. 'I wonder what Drogan and Wogon managed to agree with the Last Hope's commander … if they made contact. They're due to join us here in a few days.'

'There are good reasons to think they'll have been rejected, at best. Killed for betraying the station's position, at worst,' replied Kerensa. 'But if they have led the Centaurians to the outpost, it would be in their interests to help us, if only for their own survival. Anyway, there's only a short while before we find out. Either way. I wish we could communicate, but it isn't safe. Any transmission would reveal we aren't alone.'

Less than 48 hours later, two ships suddenly materialised alongside the Endeavour in its orbit round Pluto. They just appeared. No detectable approach, no message, nothing.

One was the Majestic, the first time they'd seen it. It dwarfed them by a magnitude of one hundred. The second craft was of a design they'd never seen before – and even larger than the Majestic. It was huge. Since it was accompanying their colleagues from Ganymede – she'd never considered Drogan a friend – Kerensa decided they must be allies. Not that there was much she could have done had they been hostile.

They had little time to wait before contact was established. There was no radio message, no flashing lights using the old Morse code. Simply a small vessel departing the larger ship, the words New Hope emblazoned along its side. It moved towards the Majestic, remaining for only a few moments before taking the short journey to Endeavour. It flew behind them and extended a massive docking sleeve towards them which completely enveloped their blunt back end. Once engaged and airtight, a knocking on the vast back door indicated they should open it.

Kerensa, Evelyn and I were waiting in what had become our training area, while a cautious Pakeman watched from the balcony with a weapon – just in case. He couldn't, of course, shoot any traitorous human, but could destroy any androids attempting to board us. He had orders to attempt firing towards each person as they entered the Endeavour, as a test of their humanity. They'd never know.

Five people entered from the other ship. Drogan and Wogon from the Majestic and three others. They introduced themselves as Commander Adjara, who commanded the vessel, Major Xing who led their troops and a military captain, Neuman, overseeing the two-man fighter ships.

Commander Adjara was a striking woman of perhaps two hundred. Her lived-in features reflected her age and experience, but she had a presence which made even the pugnacious Colonel Wogon defer to her. It was she who initiated the discussion.

'We've been sent by the leader of our outpost to help you destroy the android vessel currently passing through the solar system. We know you led them here – perhaps inadvertently – but that is no longer of any moment. Their presence is a threat to us, as well as to other Mars settlements. We have no choice in this matter. In return for our help, you will be required to leave the solar system and never return.'

143

Her harsh words took time to sink in. I was effectively being banished from my home – the cradle of all humanity. It would become a completely dead world. Arguably, it already was, since I'd left. How they would ensure compliance was academic, since we were unlikely to survive the coming conflict.

Chapter 22 – A plan comes together

'How did you get here without us noticing?' asked Kerensa, still officially in charge of the mission, although the presence of a senior representative of the Last Hope made this a moot point which would hopefully not lead to disagreement. We were making our way to the control room/conference centre. If any of our visitors were surprised by Eddie's presence, nobody mentioned it. Perhaps they were familiar with mobile robots.

'I see no reason for concealing anything from you. As a member of your settlement's council, I'm sure we can rely on your discretion – and that of your colleagues.' Commander Adjara looked slowly around we four, Pakeman having completed his clandestine task and joined us by now. We each nodded our assent.

'Thank you. The reason we haven't been discovered by the Centaurians is not solely our strategic positioning. We have also developed cloaking technology which allows us to hide our presence from all but the most targeted and minute observation. Naturally, it is a simple matter to apply this to our smaller vessels and we've taken to moving about this part of the solar system frequently, seeking essential resources. This technology has been retrofitted to the Majestic and all its fighter ships.' She nodded at Lieutenant Commander May, who smiled a confirmation. Her team of sixteen tiny craft were now effectively invisible. 'Naturally Captain Neuman's larger force of our two-man craft is already similarly equipped. We can do the same for you.'

Evelyn had been thinking rapidly, while the commander spoke. She was reviewing our outline scheme for an attack including three vessels, plus the one-man fighters we knew Majestic carried. This information made a difference.

'Commander,' she said without consulting Kerensa –
tactics were, after all, her remit. 'I suggest we don't cloak
this vessel. We could lead the attack as a visible craft. The
last thing they will expect is for us to be accompanied.'

'My dear young woman,' replied Adjara, 'what you are
proposing is suicide. They would blow you out of the
heavens as soon as you got in range.'

'Perhaps not, ma'am. Our research indicates this ship
could return to the android vessel on its own, given certain
circumstances. If we can replicate these, we would be
drawn into their docking bay before the Centaurians are
aware of anything untoward. Any cloaked vessels
accompanying us would thereby safely gain access to their
ship and help us take down their defences.'

Adjara considered the suggestion.

'How would we know the layout of their ship, to
infiltrate it and destroy their weapons?'

'My Earth-built robot has reverse engineered a schematic
of much of their ship from the tracking equipment they'd
left in this vessel,' I said, wanting not only to establish my
place in the mission – and to remind people that Earth was
far from being a spent force. (Whatever the truth might be.)

'That's interesting, but what about the parts of the ship
you don't know about?'

'As far as we can calculate, the unknown areas are
simply their propulsion system and storage facilities for the
androids when not in operation,' said Evelyn, loyally
backing me up. 'Eddie, as we call the robot, has been
invaluable to us.'

Adjara smiled at her. 'In that case, what are the
conditions which would allow you to return to their ship
unchallenged?'

'We must be dead,' replied Evelyn, her face
expressionless.

�֍

'The shuttlecraft is still in orbit round the micro-planet, called Pluto, Zoltan.' Naibu was keeping his leader fully informed. Well almost so. While watching the craft, Treban had reported a slight flicker in the readings. It somehow slipped the commander's mind to mention this to his increasingly paranoid superior. Was "paranoid" the right term for an android, he wondered in a nanosecond? It suggested emotion, which should not be possible. Yet he himself was experiencing an emotion. Doubt. About their mission, the validity of destroying an entire civilisation – even though he had played his own part in it – and, above all, about Zoltan's real agenda.

'Your evaluation, commander?'

'It has been orbiting the planet for as long as it was on Jupiter III. I suggest it is too early to determine whether they have been more effective in finding a settlement at this location. My recommendation is to await developments.'

'What of the other craft? The one exiting the system?'

'It is continuing its trajectory,' he replied simply. There was no need to confuse the admiral with facts. Such as that the nature of the signal was not *quite* the same as when first identified. Something was going on and Naibu had no idea what. But he had no intention of allowing Zoltan to destroy things without good reason.

'Are there still life-signs on the shuttlecraft?'

'It seems so, but precise readings are difficult at this range, sir. And as you know, Seguidor's signals are no longer readable.'

'Make a course for the micro-planet before we overshoot completely and have to waste time turning.'

'Yes, admiral.'

'The android ship has changed course, commander,' reported Eddie in his usual flat tone. 'It is now heading in our direction. Estimated arrival in three days.'

Evelyn had explained how we'd hidden the life-signs of the crew using the cryogenic chambers and, during training, by each person using portable bio-suppression units. Cumbersome, but no impediment. Her idea was that we should all enter stasis again, including we two who were known by the androids to be on board, leaving Eddie to oversee our return to the Centaurian ship and revive us when safely inside.

'I'm assuming they'll no longer look for bio-signs once we're inside their ship. It's a risk. But by then there will also be at least one cloaked fighter ship inside,' Evelyn had concluded. 'They'll be able to see it immediately we enter their hangar.'

Eddie's information about the course change was a timely reminder of the need to move ahead with our plans. Knowing the forces available to us, we could determine our final tactics.

Kerensa nodded at Evelyn to take the lead, then signalled Eddie to project the android ship's schematic into the middle of the room.

It was roughly spherical, although with no attempt for smoothness, since it could never enter an atmosphere. It was at least 20 kilometres across. In Earth terms, it would have reached from sea level to more than the height at which most of the atmosphere was contained. Its volume exceeded 30,000 cubic kilometres. Even allowing for half the volume being taken up by equipment, there might be space for a million androids, if densely packed. They probably didn't need much space. Conversely, there might be no benefit in having such a massive crew and operational efficiency might require only a fraction of this number. Even so there might be fifty thousand androids on the vessel; the small settler force might face overwhelming odds of fifty to one. And the androids would be defending their own base. Attacking a place of which we knew desperately little, against overwhelming odds, we'd need to be smart.

The bulk of our soldiers were from the Last Hope, but the initial assault would be led by Evelyn and me on the Endeavour.

'As you can see, for large areas we have no details,' Evelyn explained as the visitors took their time to understand the semi-transparent image. 'Can you remove the shading and make those areas, blank, please Eddie? Thanks, that's easier to interpret. Our knowledge principally covers the periphery and one or two areas deeper into the ship. But you can see this area' – she indicated a darker region near the centre – 'where the engines must be. And the section next to it is probably the control computer and communications centre. This is based on our analysis of where messages are transmitted and received.'

'I assume our objective is to take out those two areas?' asked Major Xing. Her thousand troops would lead the main part of the assault and she was interested in where they'd be headed. 'It must be at least eight clicks into the vessel.'

'That's what needs to be discussed in a formal planning meeting,' replied Kerensa, reasserting her leadership of the mission. 'Lieutenant Commander Starr has some thoughts, so I suggest we ask she, Lieutenant Colonel Wogon and Major Xing to prepare a mission plan.'

'Thank you, Councilwoman Kerensa.' Evelyn reinforced her seniority by using the formal title. 'I suggest we include the two men who will lead the initial assault team, Captain Neuman and Mr Adams, as well. But you should appoint a commander for the assault. Might I suggest Major Xing, as leader of the largest contingent?' Wogon's back stiffened, as Evelyn expected. He was titularly the most senior officer present. But her recommendation was influenced by Neuman's assessment of him as a potentially loose cannon. Brave, but not necessarily the best leader in a complex tactical situation. The colonel's fists clenched at his sides as he became the focus of attention. Yet he said nothing, simply grinding his teeth and waiting for the previously silent Drogan to defend him. Yet for reasons of his own, Ganymede's security chief said nothing. It was taken as assent and the major became de-facto leader of the battle group. But the matter of command wasn't entirely settled.

'I'm sure Commander Adjara, who leads the largest contingent in this escapade, will agree with me that Councilwoman Kerensa should have overall control of the mission,' said Drogan. 'She's the only elected representative of one of the Mars worlds present, which must supersede military rank.' Kerensa smiled as the others indicated their agreement, wondering why he was being so magnanimous, given his habitual coolness – if not antipathy – towards her.

Seven of us sat down to discuss the plan of attack. Eight, if you included Eddie, which I was inclined to do, even if he seldom provided more than factual input. In this case he was principally there to project the three-dimensional representation of the android ship. But he added comments where we might be taking an unnecessarily indirect approach.

My own inclusion within the group was a surprise to me. I had no tactical experience, although the initial suggestion had been mine. I didn't object to others taking the lead, but was pleased to be there, if only to support Evelyn.

Getting down to brass tacks, it became quickly clear how well suited Major Xing was to tactical command. She had the ability not only to think clearly about the objectives and how they might be achieved, but also to accept suggestions which improved on her own ideas without rancour. In this, Pakeman whispered to me, not quite quietly enough, she was infinitely superior to Wogon. I hoped he wouldn't pay for his indiscretion.

Chapter 23 – Stealth attack

'The course correction has been made, Commander Naibu. We will reach the micro-planet in sixty hours. What are your orders for when we arrive?'

The commander considered his deputy's question for longer than usual. It was almost half a second before he responded.

'The shuttle is programmed to assume orbit about the nearest planetoid, in the event of systems failure or a lack of command. This might be why it is there, but apparently doing nothing. If the vessel demonstrates hostility at our arrival, we must destroy it. But if the occupants are dead – which its inactivity suggests – it will return to us automatically as soon as it recognises our proximity. After recovery, we can consider our options.'

'We will do nothing then, sir. Will you inform Zoltan?'

The commander made no reply.

Kerensa, Adjara and Drogan had withdrawn from the meeting room – no doubt for refreshments – while the rest of us thrashed out the details of how best to attack the Centaurian vessel. Xing spent some time studying Eddie's schematic of the ship. As they conversed quietly, a portion of the outer shell suddenly glowed red, indicating the position of the hangar to which he had extrapolated the Endeavour would probably be towed in by a tractor beam. It was connected by a series of passageways to the computer complex and the centre of the vessel.

As Evelyn had suspected, Major Xing proved to be a good strategist. She had a solid grasp of how the force should deploy once initial contact had been made and the best way to achieve their objective, given their limited resources.

She was also a born leader, asking for suggestions before making decisions. She tactfully started with the colonel from Ganymede.

'An all-out frontal attack is best,' he claimed. 'They won't be expecting it, and the element of surprise will combat their numerical superiority. They won't be able to concentrate all their forces in one quadrant of the ship, since they won't know we're coming until the assault begins.'

Xing didn't react, but turned to the others for comment. Evelyn spoke first.

'That has merit,' she said diplomatically, 'but I wonder if there might be an alternative approach? Although we have more than a thousand troops, I don't think the initial attack can involve anything like that number. At least, not all in one location. Our position would be like a single bridgehead in an historic battle. We need to attack on more than one front …'

'… and keep a reserve to go straight for the engine, computer and communications complex.' Worryingly I was starting to finish Evelyn's sentences. I hoped this was what she had intended to say. Her smile suggested it was, but she moved on quickly.

'We'll need some engineers and computer specialists in the deep penetration squad. And someone to lead them. It can't be you, Pakeman,' she glanced at the captain, 'You need to lead the initial assault. Is there anyone suitable in the other teams?' She already knew the answer.

Grudgingly, Wogon nodded, a light gleaming in his eye as he recognised a way in which he could play a decisive role in the assault.

'I'm an engineer by training, and many of my men are specialists in computers as well as combat engineering. The rest are assault troops. I'm certain we can fight our way to the heart of the enemy vessel and destroy it.' Pakeman nodded his agreement. He knew sufficient of the officer to know his confidence was probably justified. None of them were tested in battle, but in realistic simulations, Wogon had never lost. He was a capable battlefield operator.

'I think I can help there, colonel,' said May. 'I've been looking closely at the schematics and, as Eddie might confirm, it appears there's a passage along which you might pass from the outside of the vessel directly to the computer complex. More importantly, it looks as if it's large enough for us to fly cover for you. We can work out the details later, but it could tip the balance in our favour, given their numerical superiority.'

They all looked at Eddie as if he was a human and could physically give his assent. He managed to emit a sound analogous to a cough before saying the commander was correct.

'How large are the passages, Eddie?' I asked, curious as to their possible purpose. After all, the androids were roughly the same size as ourselves, and they were unlikely to be using craft to get around. It wasn't as if they got tired. So why a channel big enough to fly through?

'My calculations indicate they are at least twenty-five metres wide, Mr Adams.'

'That's certainly enough for us to fly, turn and fight, as necessary,' said May.

'But not for our two-seaters,' said Captain Neuman from the New Hope, 'we need more space to turn. But there may be another way we can help. I'm assuming the major will be launching a separate attack from the initial assault. We can probably do our best work there.' He had worked with her sufficiently often to anticipate her likely approach.

'You're right, captain. As usual.' She smiled warmly at him, knowing his strengths lay in fighting rather than planning. But perhaps not in the way you imagine.' She had been listening to the suggestions and formulating a way of bringing them together.

'I believe we should undertake a three-pronged attack. Lieutenant Commander Starr will lead the initial assault on the docking bay with Captain Pakeman, Mr Adams and their men. I also propose sending ten of the two-man fighters immediately behind them, as support. Captain Neuman, will you place them under Evelyn's command for the mission? She'll need a competent flight leader. Have you someone?'

'Yes, and yes, ma'am,' he replied sharply, recognising he'd be leading a reduced force elsewhere.

'Thank you. The second prong of the assault will comprise of myself leading the balance of our main forces – including twenty of the two-man fighters – against another target. I've identified what appears to be a hangar about a quarter of the way round the sphere from where we believe the shuttle craft will be tractored-in. Our aim will be to create maximum disruption to their defences. We will land, supported by the fighter-craft and engage the androids in battle. At the same time, the remaining two-man fighters will harry their external defences. It'll make them think there's another wave of attack coming, elsewhere. Neuman, you must decide which of these groups you will lead and who will command the other wing.'

'Presumably, my men and I will attack at the same time, major?' asked Wogon.

'Yes, colonel, but I'm rather hoping we can get you in without your having to fight. At least initially. The route which Lieutenant Commander May identified earlier is, according to Eddie, an exhaust tube for the propulsion system. It's not the main one, so you needn't worry they'll fire it up and blow you out. We believe it's used for major course changes, rather than the main vector thrust, or minor corrections. There's no evidence of it having been used recently. It goes directly to the heart of the Centaurians' vessel.'

The balance of the day was spent refining the details as much as practical. With so little time before the enemy vessel would reach Pluto, there was no opportunity for finesse. Many decisions would have to be taken on the fly, so good communications were vital.

It was agreed that each team would have a call-sign. M for Wogon and his engineers; L for the main diversionary assault team led by Xing; E for the initial assault team led by Evelyn; and A for the attack squadron which Neuman would lead, harrying the external defences. In each case the leader would be designated as "Team letter - One" while deputies would be "Team letter - Two" and so on. This would save confusion and time in communications. In the case of the largest force, L, only officers leading each section would be identified, to avoid a proliferation of references. Anyone taking over from an incapacitated officer would adopt their call-sign.

The time for planning was soon over. Not because it was completed, but so everyone could return to their respective bio-sign suppressed vessels, prior to the arrival of the Centaurians.

For Evelyn, Pakeman and I, it was time to enter the cryogenesis machines and sleep before the initial attack.

�֎

'There has been another change in the shuttle craft, Commander Naibu,' Treban reported. 'A fluctuation in the power consumption. And we have lost any life-signs.'

'Have you checked the telemetry?'

'Yes, sir. As far as we can determine, our readings are correct. Is it possible there has been an accident? These humans seem highly fragile. Remember how difficult it was to keep the woman from the Mars space station alive for so long? There were several occasions when it looked as if her body would give out, despite being in suspended animation. We even had to replace some of her organs on several occasions.'

'I remember, Treban. I wonder if we should have implanted something in her new heart to provide us with direct readings about her condition?'

There was an infinitesimal pause.

'I thought you were aware, commander. Zoltan did put a transponder in her last heart. It is a backup in case we lose track of the craft.'

'Has anyone been monitoring it?'

'No sir, not actively. But the computer must have a log. I will investigate.'

'Good. In the meantime, I had better advise the admiral of the change. He will be pleased for something to do.'

Chapter 24 – Driving forward

As far as anyone – or anything – was concerned it was perfectly peaceful outside the Centaurian vessel. Like any android resource, it had no name, simply a designation based on the identity of its leader. In this case, it was referred to – if at all – as Zoltan-1. Its routine hadn't changed significantly for many thousands of years, but during that time, the equipment had been replaced many times. Usually, there were no changes in design. Why should there be. It was created by machines to reflect their needs and these hadn't changed in almost fifty thousand years.

What few modifications had taken place were either aberrations, caused by an overlooked error – which either increased or reduced efficiency – or as the result of hundreds of years of research. One thing which never happened was for the androids to adopt anything remotely related to human technology. It was therefore surprising that Zoltan had ever thought to extend the life of their long-term captive with a new heart, let alone one fitted with a transponder. The creation of the artificial heart had been a simple matter of necessity. The captive's feeble flesh was giving out and he wanted to keep her alive. It was a matter of expediency, not imitating humanity. Even so, at the time it had seemed a weakness, which was why he had suppressed the memory.

One area where occasional progress had been made, was in armaments. Believing humanity still pervaded this corner of the galaxy, androids had continued to refine their lethal abilities. It was, however, a very long time since they had come across any settlements to destroy and the amount of energy expended in this area had diminished. Some on the home planet were even discussing the possibility of abandoning the destruction of humankind and focusing instead on reaching out into the wider galaxy to find new challenges.

Zoltan didn't recognise the concept of challenge, however. At least, not in any context other than his desire to "challenge" the Supreme Council for overall control of the android race. He was not sure why he aimed to lead the Centaurians, simply that it was his destiny. An idea which should have set alarm bells ringing in the mind of any sentient being. Destiny was something living intelligences might aspire to; it was certainly not a logical desire for an artificial life-form driven by logic.

Although his musings were diametrically opposed to those of his deputy, their existence betrayed something which neither could easily recognise. Evolutionary convergence suggests that living beings facing similar needs and challenges – and in the same general conditions – will tend to become more similar, rather than less so, as is the case when animals adapt to different circumstances. Since androids faced problems akin to those of humanity, they were gradually becoming more 'human'. Some, like Naibu, were developing empathy. Others, like Zoltan, were becoming personally ambitious.

When his deputy entered the command cabin to report the change in conditions on the shuttle he had spent so long following his self-imposed mission to destroy what was left of humanity, he had mixed reactions. Satisfaction at the death of another human, was tinged with strong regret there would be no opportunity to follow her any longer to find more of the vermin.

'Bring the craft on board as soon as we are in range, commander,' he ordered. 'We can at least recover our watcher, Seguidor and see what went wrong with his communicator. And I suppose we might dissect the Earthman's body to see how the race there had degenerated.'

Something stopped Naibu from asking whether he should arrange for Evelyn's heart and its embedded transponder to be recovered. He didn't know what it was which stayed his words, but it seemed important, for some reason.

The tractor beam pulled the shuttlecraft Endeavour into a cavernous docking bay. The instant it crossed the threshold, two things happened. First, Eddie revived the crew. Secondly, the single android on duty in the bay became aware of the entrance of ten, previously invisible, two-man fighter craft. Not that it recognised them as such. Why should it? No Centaurian had ever seen the like before, or they would be in the database. Before it could assess the new data and react, one of the pilots had identified the android's position and fired a powerful laser beam, annihilating it.

Before the assault commenced, Kerensa, Drogan and Adjara had returned to the New Hope where they would remain for the duration of the battle. They were not far from danger, but at least the ship remained cloaked against detection. The issue would probably be irrelevant once the troops of Team L started appearing within the android ship. Lines of fifty soldiers were towed behind each of the cloaked two-man fighters towards the android ship. In addition to the bio-suppressors, which would become useless once in visual range, their spacesuits were equipped with directional thrusters and artificial gravity generators. These would enable them to be cast off near the entrance to their objective and then control their individual approach by combining thrust with negative or positive gravity, to ensure a soft landing. Well away from the main attack area, the similarly protected Team M headed towards the exhaust vent, while Team A prepared to circle the massive vessel, looking for signs of hostile fire, the source of which they could attack.

Once the assault teams were launched the Last Hope and Majestic withdrew to the other side of Pluto, for additional safety.

With no idea of the number of defenders we faced, Team E spread quickly throughout the hangar. Conversation was minimised, to prevent the androids from working out precisely how few we were. By agreed signs, Evelyn and Pakeman indicated the direction in which each soldier should go. We'd known something of the layout from detailed scans Eddie had run during the final approach, and each man had a copy of the schematic projected onto his visor, giving a context to where he was compared with the topography – and the location of other team members. Pakeman's training had been highly effective, particularly since the forecasts Eddie had produced during the last two weeks proved to be quite accurate. His final scan had simply put the flesh on a previously skeletal view.

Within minutes we'd formed a defensible perimeter within the hangar and were prepared for the next stage of Xing's plan. Guards would protect our escape route while we made a foray into the inside of the ship. Our mission was to cause maximum disruption to draw defences away from Team M. Xing's Team L had a similar mission, but expected greater resistance from the androids whose sensors must soon reveal they represented the bigger threat. This would take time and, signalling two soldiers to hold position by the Endeavour, Evelyn indicated Pakeman should take point and lead us deeper into the android lair.

The captain placed an explosive charge against the large door isolating the hangar and retired to a safe distance before blowing a hole in it sufficiently large to allow us all through. The damage would also prevent the androids from sealing it off, to prevent our escape. Passing through the opening, we suddenly found ourselves in strange surroundings. Corridors led in five directions, straight ahead, left, right, up and down. Soldiers moved two paces into each opening, testing for defences. As they entered each passage, they found themselves orientated to a different axis. On the right and left, they were suddenly walking on what had appeared to be walls, the up and down passages were similar, but the orientation was precisely the opposite; so that looking at their colleagues across the passageway was normal, but those at ninety degrees were upside down. To those remaining at the junction, it just looked strange. I laughed nervously at the sight, but Pakeman looked worried.

'We'll need to do something about this, or combat will be impossible. We might need to disrupt their artificial gravity. Shall I give a heads up to M-1?'

'They might not have the same problem, but L Team will. Yes, please tell them to disrupt it, if they can. It might also make matters more difficult for the defenders,' Evelyn decided. 'We'll keep together and head deeper into the ship. That way, at least we won't become confused amongst ourselves.'

We all moved ahead, deeper into the ship, where the gravitational orientation was the same as in the hangar. Eddie, who was silently following, suggested this might be the main axis of operation, which could make matters easier for us. He suggested the varying orientations were primarily for maintenance and access. 'There are no life-signs to estimate how many androids are aboard, commander,' he told Evelyn. 'But I am reading a mass of positronic signals approximating to the patterns I detected in the android I destroyed on Ganymede. The number is too great to count, but it seems not to be on the massive scale we had estimated. I wonder if I might find a portal to their computer, so I can try and ascertain more information.'

This suddenly became of greater moment than simply disrupting the android defences, which were remarkably absent so far. Knowing how many enemies we faced – and where they were located – would be invaluable to the other teams as well as us. Moving swiftly down the passage, constantly on the alert for opposition – even simple monitoring – we found what appeared to be a command sub-station. It was unmanned and consisted simply of a computer terminal filled with touch-screens and a keyboard. Amazingly, the androids still used very human forms of input and output. Perhaps this was a function of them seeing no benefit in – or need for – moving away from how they had been programmed to set up a new world for humanity, so very long ago.

Eddie had been constructed as a stand-alone computer to avoid contamination from other systems. He couldn't therefore simply plug himself into a port and interface directly with the mainframe. Instead he extended his legs to become the same height as an android, instead of his usual one and a half metres, and used his flexible limbs to operate the terminal. He had no problem understanding the system, which was completely logical, or accessing the information he needed. There were no security protocols. Apparently, the androids hadn't considered this necessary. After all, how would anyone other than them gain access to the computer?

❄

'Commander, we have indications of several explosions in the hangar to which the Mars shuttle was tractored. It must have failed somehow. Shall I eject it?'

'No, Treban,' replied Naibu. 'I wish to investigate. Are there any other anomalies?' He felt honour bound – another interesting concept for an artificially intelligent being – to ask, even though his instincts were to let matters develop on their own. If, as he was beginning to suspect, this was an attack on his race by the humans, he was far from certain he wanted to be responsible for repelling it. But he was an officer of the fleet and must act accordingly.

'I am not sure sir. There are unusual readings from another hangar some distance away and the automatic external defences appear to have been activated, although there is no clear indication of what the threat is. Do you wish me to send anyone to investigate?'

'No. I will go myself and then report to the admiral.' He started to move swiftly towards the turbo-lift which would transport him rapidly to the hangar, when Treban spoke again.

'Naibu,' a name he seldom used, 'someone appears to be accessing the command post computer near the shuttle craft bay. I have no record of anyone working there.'

'Thank you, Treban. I will investigate that too.' Had his deputy anticipated his intentions?

Major Xing was surprised to meet no resistance at all to their incursion. For a thousand troops and 20 fighters to assault an enemy vessel, after blowing the doors off a hangar, unopposed seemed strange. Might it be a trap? Were the enemy somehow forewarned of their arrival and be drawing them into an ambush? She selected a lieutenant and sent him with a squad of 25 to probe the defences.

'Be careful, Grover, it might be a trap. And watch out for the change in gravitational fields E-2 reported. I don't want you falling over your flat feet.' Humour under stress made her a popular leader.

Lieutenant Grover encountered a layout almost identical to that which the initial assault team had. The platoon penetrated 500 metres before encountering any resistance at all. In this case, it was disorganised, but stronger. The androids were only lightly armed, but highly disciplined and it was several minutes before they could be subdued. Had it not been for the weapons Eddie had designed for them, victory might not have been so rapid.

Grover went to check on the destroyed androids, to ensure none were still active, before setting up an advance command post and sending a runner back to Xing, asking for further instructions. No point in using communications unless it was essential.

'What do you think, Evans?' The flight-lieutenant had landed his craft, for which there currently seemed no need, and joined her for orders. He didn't expect to have his opinion sought, but responded promptly.

'There seems little point in sitting around here, major. The androids must know they're under attack by now and our mission is to enable Team M to achieve their objective. We can best do that by harrying the enemy.' Xing nodded.

'My thoughts exactly. Let's go for it. Leave half your squadron here, as a way of getting our survivors away if we run into trouble, and lead the others ahead. I and most of the troops will follow. For the moment, destroy anything which moves. We can think about intelligence gathering later, although I imagine E-1 already has that in hand. They certainly don't appear to have encountered any significant resistance.'

Chapter 25 – Into the enemy's bowels

Lieutenant Colonel Wogon was disappointed to reach the exhaust vent without incident. It wasn't a matter of wanting a fight, so much as wondering why there was no resistance. At least so he told himself. If truth be known, he'd always felt a blood-lust which constant simulated training could never satisfy. This, he felt, was his moment – or it should be. A lack of reaction from the android ship had so far deprived him of a victory. No men lost, no honour gained. He could only hope his thrust into the bowels of the ship would offer greater opportunities to prove himself.

There was no artificial gravity in the broad tube and his engineers were towed along its length by the one-man fighters at a reasonable speed. He watched constantly for any prospect of resistance, but the Centaurians seemed completely unaware of his presence. Damn them.

His earpiece, suddenly rang with fighter pilots shouting to each other in the throes of battle. At last, some evidence of resistance.

'L-1, this is A-1. We are under attack from what appears to be automated fire. We are engaging.'

'Understood, A-1. Try to keep the chatter down, if you please. L-1 out.'

'You heard chaps. Cut the cackle. A-1 silent.'

Someone had left his communicator open and it was possible for the colonel to hear occasional detonations. It was strange, he hadn't expected to hear anything in the vacuum of space. His major explained it was probably the sympathetic resonance of explosions in the pilot's cockpit. There might be no airwaves to transmit sounds, but explosions released gas which would expand rapidly and could cause vibration in nearby vessels.

Still unopposed, the small force of specialists reached the inner end of the exhaust tube. Looming ahead of them was a massive blank wall which they recognised as the source from which ions would be expelled to create thrust. To one side was a small hatch; too small for the fighter craft to navigate, but large enough for the engineers to access the engine and computer core.

'Commander May,' he said into his radio, 'we'll disembark here and proceed on foot. Withdraw as soon as we are clear, and await my call.'

'M-2 to M-1, she replied, re-establishing the correct radio protocol. 'Wilco. Good luck, sir.'

Ignorant of any rebuke, Wogon led his engineers and computer specialists into the passageway leading off the exhaust tube without the briefest look back at the fighter ships. Entering the first large space he encountered, he found a hive of activity. The room was filled with androids tending to their equipment.

'This is most interesting, Lieutenant Commander Starr,' said Eddie after scanning the computer terminal for a long time, during which the rest of us had become increasingly restless. I was concerned he was having trouble understanding what he saw. 'I apologise for the delay, but I had to check the readings because I suspected they were incorrect.'

'OK, Eddie, what have you got for us?'

'It seems that the complement of this vessel is fewer than five thousand androids, commander. Much of the space we thought might have been dedicated to housing troops for when they are needed is, in fact, sophisticated equipment supporting the most immense weapon. It is far larger than anything in my databanks and looks capable of destroying any vessel up to its own size, instantly. It could vaporise the New Hope – or even the Last Hope – in seconds. And aimed at somewhere like Ganymede, could destroy the entire settlement in the blink of an eye. This ship is designed solely to extinguish every human settlement it encounters.'

'My God.' I couldn't help it. I was completely shocked. We were inside a vessel capable of wrecking vengeance of biblical proportions on those who had originally created the androids. Evelyn was quicker to react logically.

'L-1, this is E-1. We have determined opposition will be significantly less than expected. However, Team M's success is vital to the survival of humanity.'

'Understood, E-1. That explains why we're meeting so little resistance. Can you update my visor with your intel?'

'Eddie is doing that now, L-1,' Evelyn replied, briefly wondering why they hadn't bothered to give the computer a reference number. An oversight – or a misguided attempt to avoid anthropomorphism (given he had a human name)? 'His conclusion is at the end.'

'Shit,' came a female voice in our earpieces.

'I assume that's a military term?' I asked Evelyn, hoping to lighten the sombre mood which had overtaken us – and clearly affected the mission leader. She managed a weak smile. Just.

'Did you copy that to M-1?' asked Xing.

'Yes, L-1 ...'

✷

'We have intruders in the main engineering centre.' The dispassionate voice sounded simultaneously in the ears of Zoltan and Naibu. As the two senior officers, protocol was that any problems would be reported to them alone, in the first instance.

The admiral was slowly becoming aware of something untoward occurring. He had not seen his deputy for some time and was deep in thought. A flashing red light on his command screen had hardly impinged on his mind. These things happened occasionally, but never led to anything requiring his attention. Naibu was perfectly capable of handling anything. This, however, was different. Someone was using the emergency communications channel to contact him. Perhaps he should respond. Before he could do so, Naibu's voice sounded over the same communications channel.

'What is it, Yargot?' His deputy was good at remembering names, thought Zoltan, who seldom bothered – even for the chief engineer.

'A group of armed humans entered through the number seventeen exhaust tube and tried to take over the engine room, commander. They were armed, so we destroyed them. They fought for almost five seconds, but were too slow. We suffered only one casualty.'

'Did you kill them all? Are any left alive for me to interrogate, Yargot?'

'No, their bodies are weak and their reactions slow.'

'Very well. Jettison the corpses. They will tell us nothing. I am investigating another anomaly. I will report to Zoltan shortly.' The Admiral decided everything was in hand, so he returned to his musings on the end of humanity. He didn't even bother to wonder where this group had come from. That would be for later.

Naibu found his reactions slowed by distress at such senseless destruction of sentient beings. Yet he hardly broke his stride as he walked from the turbo-lift towards the computer terminal which had been accessed.

'M-1. M-1. Come in.' An edge of concern entered Xing's voice. She didn't like the leader of the Ganymede force, but respected his ability as a soldier and engineer. More importantly, he was vital to the success of their mission. If he failed, their efforts were for nothing. And it could only be a matter of time before the settlement of Ganymede and her own habitation of the Last Hope would be discovered. Their attack had revealed the existence of a powerful force of humans, which the Centaurians might have previously only suspected. Their destruction would be an android priority.

'M-1 to L-1,' came Wogon's faint voice. At least he was using protocol now. 'We've failed. All men dead … too slow to react … too many of them … get M-2 out. I'm … dying …' Silence.

'We're out,' came May's calm voice over the intercom, although she must have heard of their failure. 'We'll assist Team A, pending further orders.'

Evelyn and I had heard the exchange – as had everyone else. The news was devastating, but particularly to those few of us who'd seen the data Eddie had gathered. There were now only two leaders on the battlefield, Xing and Evelyn. Wogon was gone and our overall leader, Kerensa was out of the loop. At least for now.

I'd never seen my companion look so ashen, not even when we first met, and she was fighting Earth gravity for the first time. Evelyn stared at me for several minutes, seemingly unable to speak or even move. Yet when she finally did so, it was clear she had been thinking hard.

'We need to regroup with Xing and decide what to do next. As I see it, we can either withdraw and try again, or see if either of our groups can penetrate the target area and finish the job. At least we have Eddie to help. But I'm not at all sure what happened down there. Surely our weapons were designed to be quick fire and they couldn't have been worried any of the people there were human and held their fire?'

'I suppose it's possible the spy which Eddie destroyed was a substandard specimen and his reaction time was atypically slow. This could have lulled us into a false sense of security,' I suggested.

'Possibly, but we've already destroyed some androids here. Anyway, we now know there aren't as many on this ship as we'd feared. That must give us some sort of edge; something which allows us to take control of and disable this weapon. The problem is what to do?'

'I can still hear you, E-1,' said Xing, over our earpieces. 'I think it's time to regroup too, but with our forces divided, we still have a tactical advantage. We will simply have to develop a plan and execute it without meeting.'

'Perhaps I can help, Lieutenant Commander Starr?' said a strange voice. It didn't come over the radio.

Chapter 26 – Unexpected help

W e were so surprised at the silent arrival of a tall humanoid figure that it took time to realise one of us should have seen his approach. Had he simply materialised or did he perhaps move so quickly the human eye couldn't register it. In either case, it might explain the loss of Team M – and make our task infinitely more difficult.

'Please do not be alarmed, commander. I am Naibu, second in command of this vessel. I intend no harm to you and your colleagues, but we need to talk.'

'How did you creep up on us without being noticed?' I asked, unable to restrain my curiosity, although I realised how inappropriate the question might appear under the circumstances. Evelyn's raised eyebrow suggested she too wondered about this – from a tactical perspective.

'… creep up …?' asked the literal minded android.

'I'm sorry, Naibu, my colleague was speaking metaphorically. He simply intended to ask how you got here,' said Evelyn.

'Ah, I understand. There are passages and lifts throughout the entire ship which may not have shown up on the scans you have undoubtedly taken of our vessel. I used one of these, although not with the intention of surprising you. Quite the contrary. The last thing I wanted was to be shot with one of your weapons. They appear to have been effective in several cases. Your team in engineering were unfortunate. And poorly led. They blundered into the one area of the ship which has automatic defences built into the structure.' This explained how Wogon and his team had been so quickly liquidated.

'Commander Starr, we have met before. You may, by now, have realised you were held captive on this ship from shortly after we destroyed your mother vessel until shortly before you reached your planet of origin. We held you in stasis for much of that time, but there were occasions when we had to bring you out of suspended animation to repair various organs which were in danger of failing. The human body cannot safely be stored for limitless time. On one such occasion, we had to replace your heart. This is how I knew where you were, commander. Your reconstructed heart contains a transponder through which we can track you.'

Evelyn looked horrified, although whether this was at the confirmation she had so long suspected, that she was easily trackable, or that she had an artificial heart I couldn't tell.

'Do not be alarmed. It is many centuries since anyone other than the leader and, I learned today, my deputy, have been aware of the fact. Treban told me about it earlier and I accessed the data, to locate you. I wanted to talk.'

Evelyn didn't look reassured and I guessed why.

'Commander Naibu,' I hoped I had his rank right, he hadn't admitted to any, 'I think Lieutenant Commander Starr is concerned who else might be able to track her, just as you did. Surely both your deputy and leader can?'

'You need not worry about that,' he addressed himself to Evelyn as if intrigued to see how their unwitting emissary was holding up after such an inordinately long life. For a human. 'I deleted all the files so nobody can use the transponder. Zoltan, our leader, seems to have forgotten about the implant and Treban is likely to follow my orders.'

'Can someone tell me what's happening?' Xing's unidentified voice sounded in our earpieces. She was monitoring the conversation with growing consternation at the revelations. Naibu could either monitor our communications, or simply overheard the buzz from my earpiece – I was standing closest to him having moved to a position where, side on to him, I could operate my weapon if necessary.

173

He looked at me. 'Please tell your leader I intend no harm, my friend. I simply want to talk.' At least he couldn't track our communications, or he would have referred to me as E-3. 'I believe I know the location of your other invasion team from our internal reports. I can take you there by hidden corridors while your team remains here,' he told Evelyn. If your fighters continue to harry our external defences, it will make Zoltan think he has everything under control.'

This might be a trap. But if it was, I couldn't see how. They could probably easily destroy us, since they knew where we were, even if not our strengths and capabilities. What was this android up to? I looked at Evelyn wondering whether this was simply a ploy to get her back under their control for some reason. A furrowed brow suggested she might be having similar doubts. She should not go alone. Pakeman would be the best companion for her; he could act as a bodyguard.

'I believe you are right, Commander Naibu,' she told him after a few seconds' consideration – which must have seemed an eternity of indecision to an android. 'Mr Adams and I will accompany you to our team leader, while Captain Pakeman remains in charge here.'

✖

'Give me a status update, commander.' Zoltan's voice sounded over the general command channel used by senior officers. 'What is happening?'

'I am sorry, sir, Commander Naibu is not currently present. He is investigating an explosion in the tractor bay,' reported Treban. 'He cannot reply directly as his communicator appears to be off-line.' The deputy was more loyal to his immediate commander than the admiral – perhaps because he could understand, even shared, some of his doubts about the mission on which they were currently engaged. He was aware Naibu had deliberately disconnected his communications device, as well as the built-in transponder with which every android was equipped. Only senior officers could do this and Treban suspected he might know why he'd taken such an extreme step. It was not for him to question, anyway. At least, that would be his defence, if challenged. And he had a secret way of communicating with Naibu, if necessary.

'My monitors show some sort of ongoing disturbances in various parts of the ship, as well as outside, lieutenant commander. Find out what is going on and report to me directly, if you cannot contact the commander.'

Zoltan closed the communication and sat in his day cabin, wondering what could have caused the current disruption. It was not his place to be concerned with day-to-day matters concerning the vessel's running; that was for the commander. He was interested in strategy. And planning to destroy humanity. And to take control of the Centaurians. He was still calculating which of the two should come first. Certainly, there was ambivalence amongst his colleagues on the Supreme Council, about whether they should continue to persecute the race which had abandoned them so long ago. Some argued they were no longer relevant. But he believed they were a canker which must be expunged, if androids were to fulfil their destiny of ruling the galaxy.

Only by becoming undisputed head of the council could he guarantee to have his policies carried out. The destruction of a few more Mars settlements might well sway the waverers in his favour. There were already those who supported him, but not quite sufficient to win a vote. He failed to comprehend the incongruity of such democratic considerations within a race based on artificial-intelligence. Theoretically, a logical decision should be obvious to all – and acted upon by universal acclaim.

Lost in thought, he failed to realise he'd received no further information from Treban.

✄

Commander Naibu – he had confirmed this was his rank – led Evelyn and me through a series of passages before showing us into what he called a turbo-lift.

'Most of our people are on the same level as us, in terms of depth within your vessel,' Evelyn objected. Even now she feared a trap, although Naibu had given us no real cause for suspicion.

'Yes, but they are a sixth of the way round the circumference. That is ten of your miles. Unless you want to walk all the way, it will be quicker for us to use this. It travels in all directions, not just inwards to the centre of the ship. We can be with your friends within two minutes.'

I didn't find this reassuring. We'd be travelling at an average speed of 300 miles an hour. Allow for acceleration and deceleration and the maximum speed we reached could be phenomenal. Best not to think about it.

We exited the turbo-lift some way from the corridor in which Team L were waiting. Naibu had pinpointed their position exactly, although we didn't then discover how. He made no attempt at stealth, pausing after the door had opened to ensure Xing and her troops were aware of our arrival. Even so we exited the lift to find ourselves surrounded by a semicircle of soldiers whose weapons pointed directly at us.

Careful to make no threatening moves, Naibu identified Xing as the leader from her rank insignia, recognising her as a major. To my surprise, she came smartly to attention and saluted him. He returned the compliment. Nevertheless, he remained the target of at least thirty fully-charged weapons.

I am not able to surrender this vessel to you,' he told Xing, after Evelyn had introduced them. 'But I can offer myself. I am your prisoner. I hope you will permit me to be of assistance to you?'

Xing looked at him suspiciously. Then at Evelyn and me. I could tell she was wondering why she should trust any of us. One enemy and two supposed allies – one from Earth – who had brought him into the main body of our force. It was clearly possible he intended us harm. Perhaps by exploding himself to destroy us; perhaps by leading us all into a trap. For some reason she couldn't understand, Evelyn at least seemed to trust him. It didn't matter what I thought; I had no influence. Yet it was clearly possible someone who had been held by the Centaurians for so very long might be under their control in some way. It could even be, I realised, that the entire sequence of events since Evelyn first landed on Earth might have been a charade aimed at bringing us to the ship on which she'd been held.

Shit.

Had I been fooled? Had we all? More importantly, how could we tell, other than by trusting this android. By which time it might be too late.

Chapter 27 – Curious behaviour

'I realise you have no reason to trust me, Major Xing. And that I might be exerting influence over your colleague who was, for so long, our prisoner. It is we who destroyed her mothership and have participated in the elimination of many other human settlements and space stations. I can only express my regret for what has happened and offer an olive branch. Although one which will not bring immediate peace.'

It took some time for any of us to realise how anomalous his sentiments were for an artificial life-form. First amongst us appeared to be Evelyn, the person who had most reason to mistrust – even hate – this creature for killing her mother and numerous friends.

'Your words are very strange, Naibu. You speak as if you might empathise with those you've killed; claim to regret their destruction. Yet surely you were only acting in accord with your programming.' My companion deliberately sought to goad him, not just with the "I was only following orders" defence once common on Earth to excuse war crimes, but also by belittling his ability to reason and think independently.

Unable to smile, he managed to convey his acquiescence by emulating the shrug he had seen colonists do just before being killed, as an indication of their acceptance of fate. It was somehow grotesque and yet meaningful. I must admit, it impressed me as no words could have.

'You are right, Evelyn; if I might call you by the name we used when you were our captive? Androids should not be capable of "emotions". Yet here I am. Someone who now questions the mission we are committed to, serving under a leader who is driven by ambition. Another thing of which we should be incapable. I am here because I do not believe it is right for us to destroy humanity. Indeed, the original impetus to do so, all that time ago, represents the naissance of a level of sentience within us which our creators – the people of Earth – could never have imagined. It became driven by a desire for revenge against those who sent us four light years away and then failed to follow. They deprived us of a purpose, and thereby allowed us to develop one of our own.'

As he spoke, I noticed several of the weapons trained on him starting to droop. Was this, I wondered, the result of mesmerism, of the soldiers being lulled into a false sense of security. Or could it be their recognition of the vulnerability – dare I say the humanity – of this robotic figure which had placed itself in our power. For each soldier believed he or she could destroy it in a second.

One of the greatest challenges facing any leader is to know when inaction is preferable to action. Xing could easily have ordered the soldiers to fire. It wasn't as if Evelyn and I could be struck by projectiles from these modified weapons. Yet she could also accept the possible truth of what Naibu said – or at least his belief in it – and grasp what he had so graphically (and anachronistically) described as an "olive branch".

Silence lengthened and deepened for several minutes – which must have been an eternity to the android – before our tactical leader spoke.

'What do you suggest we do now, commander? Can you lead us in an attack to destroy this vessel?'

Naibu responded without hesitation.

'Not as such, lieutenant commander. You cannot hope to penetrate the ship quickly enough to overcome our defences; not since the death of your men in engineering. I would like to talk with your leaders, so we can decide on a way of bringing peace between our two races. For I believe we have become as close to a race as it is possible to be. We are self-aware, intelligent and capable of self-reproduction, albeit in a different manner from you. I would argue we are alive and that we should each respect the other for that.'

'What then?' asked Xing.

'The leader of our vessel will never accept peace. Nor will some of its officers, although my deputy, Treban, will support me. If you agree, I believe we should withdraw to a place of safety, allowing Zoltan to believe you are defeated – and I am destroyed. It is obvious to me that you must have a way of disguising your vessels from detection, so we can repair to whatever mothership you have nearby and discuss the future. Treban will ensure our ship does not move from here for some time.'

Xing withdrew with Evelyn, the two surviving tactical leaders discussing their options. For me it seemed sensible to accept Naibu's offer of mediation, but I knew our withdrawal would be complicated. And there was no chance of communicating with the New Hope, for fear of betraying its location. It was a decision only the two women could take.

'Do you think we can trust him, Evelyn?' asked Xing. 'You must hate him more than most. Yet you seemed inclined to give him the benefit of the doubt.'

'I suppose it's a matter of hope, Wu.' It was the first time she'd used Xing's given name. Few people bothered with them, except within the family. 'Mother never hated anyone, not even my father,' a distant memory forcing a smiled to her eyes. 'But she never came across the androids until they destroyed her ship. Yet I believe she would want me to try and bring about peace – if possible. Humanity has had its share of violence and killing, since the dawn of time. But what has it really achieved? We have enjoyed greater scientific progress through space exploration than all the wars ever fought. If we are being offered a genuine opportunity to end the persecution of our race by these Centaurians, we should grasp it with both hands …'

'… and even if it isn't genuine, the worst we can do is bring forward the date of our destruction, given what we know of their prowess in hunting us down.' Wu Xing completed the thought for her. 'Give the order for withdrawal, lieutenant commander.'

Withdrawal was a complex matter. Team A had lost several fighters to the android defences and Team M consisted only of the support fighters. The other teams had suffered few casualties, and everyone evacuated the same way they had arrived. Except for Team E. Removing the Endeavour from within the tractor bay was impractical and would have warned Zoltan of something serious occurring. Evelyn arranged for the 2-man fighters which had been supporting Team A for want of anything else to do, to tow Eddie, Pakeman and the remaining soldiers in his platoon away, in the same way everyone else had arrived. With all craft cloaked, and the soldiers' life-signs suppressed, the assault effectively ended as suddenly as it had started.

�֎

'Zoltan,' said Treban into his communicator. He knew what Naibu was doing thanks to a private communication from his commander once the evacuation had been agreed. 'The disturbances have ceased. It appears a small group of humans somehow gained access to the ship and did limited damage. All have been destroyed.' He didn't expect the Admiral to ask about casualties. He wouldn't care. But he needed to report one.

'I regret to advise you that Commander Naibu appears to be amongst the few androids destroyed. He was investigating the disturbances and we lost contact with him.' Almost true.

'Congratulations on your promotion, Commander Treban,' was all Zoltan said.

Treban closed the connection without, of course, displaying any emotion. Did he feel any? He wasn't sure. He wondered precisely what Naibu was doing. Certainly, the commander had not been destroyed; but neither, he was sure, was his former chief still on the ship. This could mean only one thing. Naibu had defected to the humans, for some reason of his own.

The two androids had never discussed their attitude towards the persecution which was being visited on the Martians, but comments which occasionally passed between them suggested neither was in sympathy with what was being done – perhaps more by Zoltan than any other leader. Naibu had once described a slowing of his positronic brain functioning whenever ordered to perform an act of destruction, only alleviated by some small act of mercy which he subsequently managed to undertake. If that was the case, thought Treban, Naibu must now be finding his circuits running more smoothly than ever before. There could be little doubt who was behind the successful withdrawal of the human assault force.

What was more difficult to understand was how Zoltan could be so ignorant of events. Could he really be so blinded by his own hatred of humanity as to be unaware of the undercurrent of doubt amongst some officers? Conversely, many others were apparently as vehement in their hatred of the Martians as their leader. Perhaps, like so many autocrats, he was only able to hear those voices which supported him. The emperor will only ever know he has no clothes, if someone stands up to tell him. With Naibu gone, would this role now fall to Treban?

Returning to the New Hope and Majestic took longer than the initial assault because they remained hidden the other side of Pluto. The original plan had been for Xing to send a signal indicating their success, at which point the Majestic was to come and collect them without danger of retribution from the stricken android ship. Had the mission failed, there would have been nobody to recover, anyway. Even so, it was less than six hours before the procession of small craft towing linked lines of space-suited soldiers and a single unsuited android, to reach its objective. If Zoltan had anyone to look carefully, they would have noticed nothing except the occasional flash of light from an engine or control panel. All craft and space-suits were bio-suppressed and Naibu had no active transponders. He had even electronically deactivated Evelyn's, just in case there was a backup tracking system of which Treban had been unaware.

Chapter 28 – Council of war

W e all returned to the New Hope, the smaller Majestic largely acting as an overflow, when needed. Councilwoman Kerensa, Commander Adjara and Security Chief Drogan had been in constant conference since the departure of their forces half a day – or half a lifetime – earlier, although there had been little to discuss. They'd monitored the occasional cryptic messages, but apart from being aware of the loss of Wogon and his team – and the consequent failure of the mission, they knew nothing.

We entered the New Hope's spacious conference room, a place with which only Major Xing amongst us was familiar. The generous space – indeed the entire ship – was a revelation emphasising the smallness of our – now lost – shuttlecraft. The room seemed large enough to rival anything on Ganymede, although logic suggested this was unlikely. We were led in by armed guards, who presumably reported to Commander Adjara or Wu Xing, and I could see space to seat at least thirty people around an oval table. The commanders of the vessels were together on one side of the table, while we were directed opposite. Naibu sat between Evelyn and me, while Xing flanked me. Eddie, who had somehow entered virtually unnoticed, stationed himself behind. Several of the guards retreated to the walls, whilst others withdrew altogether.

Kerensa presided over the triumvirate, even though not the host.

'Welcome back, Major Xing, Lieutenant Commander Starr and Mr Adams. Who, may I ask, is this?' She must have had a good idea. It was Evelyn who answered, as she'd previously agreed with Xing.

'Councilwoman, commander, security chief, may I present Commander Naibu of the Zoltan-1 – the Centaurian vessel we've been monitoring, while they tracked my shuttlecraft. He's an android,' she added, perhaps unnecessarily. 'I wish to reassure you he is not transmitting any signals to his ship and is no longer prepared to serve in it. He is here to help us.' There was an almost audible indrawing of breath. Was this surprise, I wondered? Or a manifestation of some ancient belief that humanity was superior to its creations, which should naturally eventually fall in with our commands? Or was the Frankenstein-complex too deeply ingrained within us, for such an assumption to be made?

In addition to the seven participants – eight if you included Eddie, which I was inclined to do – only a handful of guards remained. Kerensa spoke quietly to Commander Adjara, who looked at the guards and addressed them directly.

'Sergeant. You and your men will forget what you've just heard. You will remain in this room, but nothing which takes place is to be spoken of outside it without my express permission. Proceed, Lieutenant Commander Starr.'

'Commander Naibu was not responsible for the failure of our mission. Our incursion into the engine room was met by automatic defences to which we had no reply. Colonel Wogon and his men were wiped out within seconds. It was not his fault; he acted bravely. Naibu became aware of the nature of our incursion and came personally to lead us to safety. It was impossible for us to reach the engine room and destroy it, once the colonel's team was spotted and neutralised. Naibu facilitated our escape by temporarily disabling some of the ship's monitoring systems. He also gave us important intelligence in addition to what we'd gathered ourselves. Perhaps he might speak for himself, with your permission?'

The three senior officers nodded their assent, and Naibu rose to address them. He was an impressive – if also impassive – figure. Strong, but impossible to read, which made it uncomfortable to watch him; never knowing whether he was telling the truth or not. His first words didn't help, either.

'I was not entirely honest with your officers, madam councilwoman. I rightly told them they had no chance of reaching their objective, but I didn't explain why. The officers and crew of Zoltan-1 outnumber you significantly, but that is not the only issue preventing the success of your mission. Critical devices within the vessel are specifically designed to require an artificial intelligence to operate them. However sophisticated, the human brain will not suffice. Even we must act two at a time to perform certain key functions. These include the protocols which will disable the weapon at the heart of the vessel, identified by your robot.' He indicated Eddie. 'It correctly estimated its power as sufficient to destroy this vessel – and many larger – as well as small moons and planets. It is the deadliest in a series of similar ships developed since we first came across your people on Lieutenant Commander Starr's mother's ship. At the time, our vessel had been working on a prototype weapon ever since first intercepting a transmission from it. The "Decimator", as it is called, has been upgraded many times since then.'

Nobody was sure whether this was bravado, or the truth. Yet what reason might Naibu have for lying to us?

'There is only one chance for you to avoid rapid annihilation by my kind,' the android continued. 'You must destroy the Zoltan-1 completely. I am confident its captain, Zoltan, will not have mentioned this encounter to the high council on Centauri. There are political ramifications which I need not outline now, but he will not wish to admit even the fact of an enemy incursion onto his vessel before he can also report your complete eradication. The Decimator is close to the engineering centre you so skilfully reached. But it is contained within a gravitation-free vacuum, filled with radiation at very high levels, and is protected from even the largest explosion on the ship itself. To destroy it, you must get inside and trigger an explosion manually.'

His words left us deeply thoughtful. I hardly noticed when he sat down. Our mission had never really had a chance of success. Even blowing up the engines would not have destroyed the ship - probably wouldn't have damaged anything on the opposite side of the ship to where the explosion was set. We would have remained sitting ducks for retaliation.

'What do you suggest, Commander Naibu?' asked Kerensa quietly.

The android stood again, as if better able to express himself from the erect position.

'There is really only one option, madam. I and another of my kind must enter the central chamber and activate the mechanism manually ... with a zero-range target. This will lead to the obliteration of the entire ship virtually instantaneously. You must remain this side of this planetoid, or you also will be destroyed.'

'But that will kill you and your colleague – if you can find one to volunteer, commander. Do you care so much for us and so little for your own survival?' challenged Adjara.

'My survival is a matter of little importance compared with what I believe. You may find such a statement at odds with everything you might assume about artificial intelligence. Belief is a concept which should be alien to me. Yet self-awareness has altered the way some of us think. Not all, of course. For most of our race – if I might call us such – existence comprises solely of fulfilling their programming and following instructions. Yet some have found the leisure – and discovered the ability – to think in more abstract terms about our place in the universe. For some – such as Zoltan and many of his Supreme Council colleagues – this has become a desire to destroy humanity, to prevent them polluting the galaxy …'

'… that's the precise expression used just before the attack on us in the Maris,' Evelyn couldn't prevent herself from interjecting, turning white at the memory.

Instead of talking over her interruption, as many men might have done, Naibu stopped and looked at her. He was already aware of her family background – the loss of her mother in their attack – and was forming a bond with her closer than she allowed many men to have. Had he been able to do so, I'm sure he would have given her a reassuring smile. As it was he simply apologised.

'Evelyn, I am so sorry for what was done to your friends and family. I was a more junior officer when Zoltan launched his unprovoked attack on you. There was nothing I could do to prevent it.' He paused, then turned back to face the senior officers again.

'To stop humanity from "polluting the galaxy" has become something of a mantra amongst the hawks within the council. Yet many of us disagree, believing we should – and can – work together with those who created us to move out into the galaxy together; working in harmony for our mutual benefit. I am one such, but have no foothold on the Supreme Council. But I understand it contains at least one or two like-minded individuals. If we can convince them to speak out, it might be a start.'

'Surely then, your personal survival is essential to our long-term security, Commander Naibu,' said Drogan. I'd long suspected he had little experience of battle, and none of self-sacrifice. Or perhaps I simply didn't like or trust him.

'I will record a message for those whom I know I can trust, to be delivered by others, sir. Presently, it is more important to secure your ship's survival than mine. My sacrifice will be an earnest of good faith.'

�֍

Treban stood in the command room, slightly behind Zoltan, in the deputy's traditional position. His mind wandered to where he imagined Naibu might now be and what he could be doing. His erstwhile commander's message had been so cryptic. He would certainly be planning something to further the dreams which he now recognised they shared, to foster peace between humanity and androids.

How easy would it be, he wondered, to destroy the evil-minded, power-hungry, megalomaniac sitting in front of him? Could he bring himself to end the life of another intelligence, or would that make him as bad as the monster Zoltan had become? For now, all he could do was obey such orders as were essential, while seeking to frustrate any which might lead to more needless deaths.

Zoltan seemed more incensed at the fact of an incursion into his domain than its broader implications. He had long believed there must be some humans left to offer resistance – it was why he had initially pressed for this mission and sustained it through so long. Having found some of the hated species, he wanted to annihilate them. That they had infested his own vessel was insupportable, and it involved wasteful circular thinking about matters over which he had no immediate control. Inefficient.

Yet the humans had managed to approach unseen. Something he could act on. He turned to Treban.

'Commander. You will set a team to discover how the human scum managed to disguise their vessels. Also, destroy one in ten of the monitor-guards on duty prior to the attack. They must have been negligent.' Treban was horrified. It would mean terminating as many as five android brains. Could he do so, or was there a way to emulate Naibu's bravery by protecting them? He would have to think.

189

Chapter 29 – One last push

Kerensa asked Naibu to withdraw, suggesting I should accompany him, taking Eddie with us. My mobile computer hadn't participated in the discussion – it would have been inappropriate – although I guessed he must have an opinion. It was a pity we couldn't stay with Evelyn and Xing to continue what was likely to be a lively debate about whether to trust Naibu. My vote would be "aye", but it didn't count in this forum, since I only represented myself and a dead planet. The others were all, effectively, from Mars. Had I been dismissed as an irrelevance, or sent to watch over our visitor? Perhaps a little of each. Anyone could guard Naibu, but having me accompany him rather than a soldier might have been as a courtesy; treating him as a guest, rather than a prisoner.

Not knowing the layout of the New Hope, I asked Eddie whether there were any observation ports through which we could view Pluto. Rapid reference to the ship's computer directed us towards a rest area which offered refreshments and a massive window looking in the direction of the micro-planet, I'd specifically avoided asking for an eatery, knowing it would be of little value to Naibu. Now Eddie had mentioned food, I noticed a gnawing hunger within me. It was many hours since we'd eaten.

Naibu, Eddie and I found an elevator which would take us to the correct level and walked amongst the crew unmolested, although they must have wondered about my companion. It wasn't a matter of his appearance which might draw comment, but something in his demeanour which suggested inflexibility and lack of emotion. Of course, his construction didn't allow for a display of feelings, so his face would always appear impassive. Yet I was beginning to detect something in our new ally which suggested hidden depths which occasionally manifested themselves in subtle gestures and sounds.

As we neared the rest area, we were immediately approached by a uniformed stewardess who asked if she could help us. I looked at Naibu, uncertain about how he would react to my eating when he patently couldn't. I needn't have worried.

'Thank you miss,' he said to the short blond-haired woman. 'I do not require anything except a seat from which I can view this planet. My friend, however, would like to see your menu and order refreshments.' We were shown to a table – Eddie resting to one side, apparently looking out of the window – while another steward brought over the menu.

'You knew I was hungry?' I asked.

'It was a guess, based on the length of time you have been exerting yourself and the noises coming from your stomach. I must admit, I have also studied what little I could about your culture and understand the need for regular meals, relaxation – including sleep – and constructive activity. I have come greatly to admire humanity.' Naibu demonstrated surprising curiosity; something I hadn't expected in an android. I had much to learn about my progenitors' creation.

It seemed appropriate to tell him something of myself, so I explained how I came from a different background from the others, being from Earth, rather than a Martian settlement. He seemed interested in the decline of my civilisation and I saw no reason to obfuscate what was, in my view, an uninspiring end to our history. He was too sensitive to offer conclusions about where we'd gone wrong, but I sensed he was keen to say something, so I probed.

'If I may say so, the story you outline is one of a race losing its sense of identity; its reason for existence. Your people seem to have ceased to strive, instead considering achieving what you described as "Nirvana" – and an incorporeal existence – as a suitable objective. Yet you personally are different. If you were like other Earth people, you would not have abandoned your comfortable home and embarked on what might be a perilous undertaking. Why?'

I got the impression he wanted me to challenge myself, my motives, rather than simply to explain.

'I could say it was fear that you might attack my planet – we were beginning to suspect you might be following Evelyn. It would be understandable for me to leave home simply out of self-preservation, I suppose. On the other hand, I might pretend to a chivalry I don't possess; that I wanted to help a young woman in distress. But if I'm honest, I think I was becoming bored with being the last person alive, as far as I was aware. The opportunity given me by a shuttlecraft from Mars allowed me to do something, rather than waiting for death to bring humanity to a slow end, in another hundred or so years.'

Naibu sat quietly while I ate a plate of uninspiring looking food, accompanied by a mildly alcoholic (but extremely tasty) beverage. He didn't say anything further until I'd finished.

'I believe you are deceiving yourself, Mark Adams. Your actions, so far as I have seen, are similarly motivated to my own. You do not follow a course of self-aggrandisement, nor, as far as I can see, are you expecting any reward for your actions. Yet you remain with Lieutenant Commander Evelyn Starr, faithfully supporting her, at no small risk to yourself. I suspect you believe there is something better for humanity, as I do for android-kind. Your willingness to place trust in me – far more quickly than others – suggests you share my vision of our two races being able to move forwards together. I wonder if this is because it was your direct ancestors who sent my predecessors to Alpha Centauri so long ago?'

Shortly after we'd lapsed into a companionable silence –
me looking through the windows at a micro-planet I'd never
expected to see, Naibu thinking inscrutable android
thoughts – Evelyn came to find us. It was easy enough for
her to do so, she simply asked if anyone had seen Eddie.
Robots like him were a rarity in most Martian cultures.

'No, thanks, I've already eaten with Wu Xing and the
others,' she replied when I offered refreshments. 'I wanted
to let you know the outcome of our deliberations.'

The options were probably limited, I'd realised. Either
we worked with Naibu to destroy his ship, or we turned tail
and ran – perpetually to be hunted down until what
remained of our kind were destroyed. Doing what with him,
I wondered?

'We've no option but to take decisive action. Contacting
the Last Hope for instructions is too dangerous and we
represent, between us, three separate groups of Mars
descendants – and one from Earth.' That she included me
carried a significance I missed at the time. 'It has been
decided we will follow Naibu's lead and try to destroy the
enemy vessel by attacking the weapon which might
otherwise pick off our settlements one by one.'

She turned to look at Naibu.

'Commander, we would like to take up your offer of
leading the attack. Four of us will join you, Major Xing,
Captain Pakeman, Mr Adams – if he agrees – and me. We
can also take Eddie.' I was secretly delighted not to be
excluded from the final phase of our adventure. Though
whether this was bravado, or a desire to see matters through
to the end – or something else – I wasn't sure.

'We need another android, to make this work,' replied
Naibu, his commitment beyond doubt. 'I am confident my
former deputy will help. Even at the cost of his own
destruction. He shares my views.'

'But how will he be able to help us?' I foresaw difficulty in relaying any instructions to him without compromising our position through conventional communications.

'I believe that will not be difficult, Mark, Evelyn,' unusually, he used our first names, nodding to each as he spoke them. 'Before I left the Zoltan-1, I created a small subroutine and inserted it in Treban's positronic software. It will not influence him – that would be wholly unacceptable – but it allows us to communicate. I will tell him what is required, and he can update me with progress. But first, we must have a detailed plan and I suggest the six of us go somewhere private.' That he included Eddie amongst us was, perhaps, logical.

Treban selected the five androids to be destroyed on Zoltan's orders with great care. Those out of the fifty-strong team which had failed to spot the incursion would be aware how easily they might have been included in a decimation, deactivating one-in-ten of a cohort. Selecting five known troublemakers would enable him to intimidate the others into taking more care in future. More importantly, it also enabled him to isolate androids who had shown the ability to think independently; something unacceptable amongst the crew.

He led them to the tractor bay in which the Endeavour still rested, telling them to stand to attention in line, in front of it.

'Your execution is being observed not only by your own colleagues, but by every android on the ship. It must be understood that negligence is as great a crime as dereliction of duty, or deliberate disobedience. Our leader, Zoltan, will shortly give the order for you to be deactivated by laser beam to the brain, whereupon your remains will be fired into space in the enemy vessel standing behind you. It is the final ignominy for your gross failure.' Normally defunct androids were recycled.

He stood to attention and saluted, the signal he had agreed with Zoltan to press the button which would execute the miscreants. As Zoltan closed the circuit, the flash of five laser beams simultaneously searing into five android heads momentarily blinded the monitors. All fell to the ground and, by the time the crew could see the punishment site again, all five androids lay inert on the hangar floor.

Treban paused for several minutes, allowing the impact of this punishment to impinge on every mind on the ship, before giving the signal for the remote viewing to be ended. He directed two crew members from the same cohort to load the inert bodies into the Endeavour. Once done, he dismissed them and entered the craft behind them, symbolically shutting the door on this despicable chapter of Centaurian history.

Once unobserved inside, the commander settled the inert bodies into the cryochambers in which the attackers had disguised their bio signatures. Not that this was necessary for androids, but it was somewhere convenient to store them.

He then reactivated one of the androids he'd just 'destroyed'.

'I am sorry you had to experience that Sergeant Chukka. As I warned you, Zoltan insisted on an example being made of your cohort and it was an opportunity to remove you and the others from duty, so we could decide on how to assist Commander Naibu.'

'Understood, commander. I did not warn the others in case anyone spoke out of turn. I am confident, however, that they share our views. They are loyal to the commander and you anyway. What are your orders now?'

'I must return to duty immediately, In the meantime, I want you to take this vessel out of the tractor bay and away from here. There is a micro-planet nearby, go there and explode the device you will find over there.' He pointed to a corner of the cabin. 'It will create the impression you were crashed into it as a final punishment. You can land and await my orders there. I will communicate with you using a beam targeted towards the location of the explosion. Be ready.'

Chapter 30 – The final attack

'I don't see how we get into the ship this time,' I said. Five of us, plus Eddie, were meeting privately to discuss our ideas. We knew we must reach the super-weapon so Naibu and (hopefully) Treban could destroy it from inside. Unfortunately, we were on the opposite side of Pluto to their ship with no obvious way of reaching it. We could approach as before, our life-signs and vessel signatures obscured, but Naibu assured us there would by now be additional defences capable of preventing actual ingress.

'I believe Treban will be able to help us there,' replied Naibu. 'My former duties, which he has now taken over, include monitoring the external defences. Had I not defected, I imagine I would have been censured for the failure to detect you, anyway. I will communicate with him again now and agree an approach which will not cause concern. I have an idea which might work, but must discuss it with him first.' He declined to comment further, perhaps fearing his plan might prove impractical.

We expected him to withdraw to contact Treban. Instead, he simply sat still, as if deep in contemplation. After no more than a few minutes, he became animated again – as far as that could ever be applied to him.

'I was right to leave. Five of the monitoring crew who reported to me have been destroyed for negligence, as a warning to the others. As their commanding officer, I would undoubtedly have been amongst them, had I remained. Treban is firmly with us. All the way. I must find an alternative method of communicating with the Supreme Council. I had intended to use him, but he insists on being with me at the end. Loyalty at this level is a new concept amongst us.'

He went on to tell us what Treban had arranged for those selected for termination and how he was confident we might rely on them to help execute our plan. The new commander also had an idea about how we could reach the Zoltan-1 unobserved ... or at least unsuspected.

It took him half an hour to explain a conversation which had lasted less than five minutes between the two androids.

Elsewhere, another discussion was taking place on the New Hope. Councilwoman Kerensa and Security Chief Drogan were deep in discussion. It was far from friendly.

'Your incompetent leadership of the mission led to its failure – and the death of a valued and highly experienced soldier, not to mention other casualties, Kerensa. I shall report this to Leka on our return to Ganymede. If, that is, ever reach there again. As things stand, your foolishness has resulted in us being in danger of our lives and unable to move anywhere for risk of being observed and followed back to the habitation. This has been a disaster.'

Kerensa might have been taken aback by this verbal assault, had she not already harboured suspicions of the ambitious Drogan. His wish to secure his own place on the council was of longstanding and she suspected his championship of her to lead the mission was largely because he believed she would fail, thereby creating an opening for him. Had they succeeded, he would undoubtedly have found a way of diminishing her role and enhancing his own – aided, no doubt, by the late Colonel Wogon.

She measured her response.

'Might I remind you, Drogan, it was you who wanted me to lead the assault. You were also a party to its planning. However, now is not the time for recriminations. We have been given the opportunity to succeed where, unbeknownst to us, the first mission was doomed, because of their technology.'

'Yes, Kerensa, but only by relying on one of THEM to execute some convoluted plan on our behalf. How do we know he – it – can be trusted? We know nothing of this Naibu, except that he was party to one a human being held captive for twenty thousand years. Hardly a recommendation of trustworthiness, is it?'

'Your objections are pointless, Drogan. We aren't the sole representatives of our race here; indeed, we are in a minority. And it's arguable that the crew of this vessel have a far greater interest in our ultimate success than we do. Their home is closer than ours and would undoubtedly be attacked first, should we fail. If you wish, I am sure nobody would object if you were to return to the Majestic and scuttle home to Ganymede. It is, after all, cloaked from detection. I am staying here to see this through to the end.'

For him to flee would be an indelible act of cowardice. He was effectively stymied.

'Are we agreed?' Having outlined the plan, Naibu was scrupulous in ensuring all of us were in accord regarding what we were about to undertake. It would be highly dangerous for everyone involved. The most hazardous part would be reaching the Zoltan-1. To do so, we had to retro-fit the Endeavour, which was supposed to have been destroyed and now rested on the 'wrong' side of Pluto, with the stealth technology used by the other vessels.

To achieve this, Commander May would fly one of her two-man fighters to the micro-planet's surface with an engineer onboard, while two other craft would ship the equipment to Endeavour, before returning to the New Hope. Once fully installed by the engineer and Sergeant Chukka, the Endeavour would be flown to meet us on the 'other' side of Pluto. There Naibu, Evelyn, Pakeman, Eddie and I were to embark ready for the journey – Major Xing had intended to join us, but was prevented by Commander Adjara, as being required in the control centre. I suspected it was really because she was considered too valuable to waste on a quixotic adventure – and might be more useful in the fight to come, when we failed.

One argument we lost, was over the intention to reactivate of the other four androids on the shuttlecraft. Commander Adjara overruled our wish fearing, perhaps, duplicity on their part and the risk of an attack on her vessel.

'Yes, commander,' each of us (except Eddie) agreed to Naibu's question, in turn.

'Then we must begin. I will inform Treban and give him his instructions. He is currently also our sole means of communicating with Sergeant Chukka, to alert him to Lieutenant Commander May's imminent arrival.'

It was strange seeing the Endeavour flying towards us, once it had been suitably adapted. At least, it was for me. I recalled the first time I'd seen it flying out of Earth's clear blue sky, but the frisson of excitement now was even greater. Before there'd been the thrill of meeting another person for the first time in many decades; now it was anticipation of another bout of action. I'd like to say it was bravery, but I think I was really motivated by a desire to get matters over and done with.

As soon as we embarked, Evelyn set course for the android vessel, while Sergeant Chukka accompanied Naibu to revive the four remaining android soldiers. As expected, they were confused at not having been destroyed and only when their former commanding officer and sergeant explained, did they understand what had happened. Gratitude for Treban's mercy reinforced their loyalty to Naibu – and resentment towards Zoltan. Indeed, they'd been selected largely because they were known to be unsympathetic to the regime aboard his ship and amenable to argument regarding the sense in cooperating with humans. There were probably others of the same persuasion aboard, but these would have to be sacrificed for the greater good, as part of the plan. Responsibility rested heavily on Naibu for this, but he accepted it as a necessary step towards the goal of peace.

The plan was relatively simple. Flying in a virtually undetectable craft, we would be able to get within visual range safely. Once within a dozen or so kilometres, we were susceptible to being noticed as light reflected off our hull, or we burned our engines to slow down – there would be no tractor beam this time. To minimise the risk, Treban was to run a computer drill simultaneously with our arrival, ensuring all monitors were fully engaged in checking their equipment, rather than idly looking out of the windows, or at their screens.

As soon as we were alongside, Treban would open the door to the same tractor hangar as before and we would fly in under our own steam. Detection systems within the bay would be disabled, so we should be completely unobserved.

Everything went precisely to plan. Almost too much so for Pakeman, who felt the calm was a bad sign.

'I'm never happy at this stage of a mission, commander,' he told Evelyn. 'Once the action starts I know what to do. But I find the period when everything is in the hands of others, unsettling. What if Treban didn't manage to conceal our arrival and there's a small army waiting for us?'

'Don't worry, captain,' said Naibu, who had overheard. 'Everything went perfectly. I have just communicated with Treban. He cannot meet us immediately, or his absence will be noticed. That is why our plan demands we wait at an agreed point for exactly two hours. There is a shift change then and he can disappear without comment.'

He noticed my smile and raised eyebrow.

'Yes, my friend, even androids have shifts. They are longer than I imagine humans could undertake, but we discovered a long time ago that efficiency demanded varying activity on a regular basis. Those engaged on monitoring proximity censors now will shortly move to maintaining some of the heavy equipment on the vessel, while those currently involved in maintenance will progress to combat training, or advanced calculations, or something else. It prevents the artificial intelligence from stagnating by concentrating too much on one area. You might argue it is a substitute for creativity.'

I must admit to having been surprised by this. Not so much the fact of moving between jobs, but that Naibu – and by implications others – recognised a principal difference between them and us being our ability to think imaginatively. I found this disheartening. Not for us, but for a culture where there was presumably no scope for art, music, literature or other forms of human endeavour. He must have been reading my thoughts.

'Why do you think I am so keen for us to work together, in future, Mark? You will enrich our lives, while we can help you expand further than ever before. But we have landed and must move now.'

Knowing he mustn't move too soon, Treban spent the rest of his shift alert to further contact from Naibu while carefully watching internal sensors and monitors for evidence of how the incursion progressed. No indications would be good.

For one moment, he noticed an anomaly on the route they were planning to use, the details of which he had discussed with

THE LAST MAN ON EARTH

Naibu earlier. A sensor flashed amber, indicating a possible contact with something unexpected. An alert guard drew this to his attention and he was just about to dispatch the only one of them he was confident he could trust, to investigate, when the sensor reverted to green.

'Sorry, commander,' reported the guard. 'I have run a diagnostic check and it was a power surge. I will make a report for this to be investigated during the next duty shift.'

'Well done,' said Treban. 'You are to be commended for your vigilance and speed in dealing with the matter.'

Had he been human, the commander might have heaved a sigh of relief at the escape from detection. As it was, he noticed a minor surge of power through his artificially intelligent brain.

Chapter 31 – Into the lion's den again

It was strange being on the Zoltan-1 again, this time led by one of its own officers. As we walked silently along the narrow corridors behind Naibu, I noticed a light flash once, overhead.

'Stop.' I said, as quietly as I could manage, given the shock it'd given me. 'We've been detected.' I was bringing up the rear with the sergeant and two of the reactivated androids, while Naibu and the other two led. Between us were Evelyn, Pakeman and Eddie, silently trundling along on his wheeled lower limbs.

Everyone stood still and waited. We were all armed and willing to make a fight of it, if necessary. Evelyn, particularly, dreaded being taken prisoner again. She'd once told me she didn't remember her captivity, but the thought of a further period in suspended animation was worse than being killed in action. I agreed. I may be no soldier, but I was prepared to fight for what I believed in. And this was increasingly Evelyn – and her people, of course.

Naibu stood immobile for a second or two, listening to Treban, before turning to face us.

'There is no cause for alarm. It was a detector which should not have recorded our presence. It is supposed to respond only to fire. Perhaps it was your combined body heat which confused it. It has been recorded as a computer error and will be repaired. We must move quickly, although nobody will be here for hours. Spread out more, please. There are many similar devices on our route and we do not wish to raise suspicion by leaving a trail of such events. Computers and androids are very good at noticing anomalies.' A statement of fact, rather than boasting.

We continued for what seemed half a day, but cannot have been so long, given when we were to meet Treban. I was becoming tired and hungry. So, perhaps were the others. Activity and tension can give one an appetite.

Eventually, we came to a large chamber equipped, incongruously, with a dozen chairs.

'Expecting guests?' asked Evelyn, quizzically. Androids would have no need for these, surely.

Naibu might have looked embarrassed, had it been possible. Instead he gave a convincing approximation of a shrug.

'No, commander, this is where faulty android brains are operated on. Having them seated is more convenient for the operatives to reach. I chose it for a rendezvous with Treban where you would be able to sit.' It was a small consideration, but meant more to us than he might have realised. He was about to destroy himself and his own ship for the sake of peace between our races, but could find time to consider our comfort. He was truly remarkable.

We unpacked our provisions, but ate sparingly. No way of telling how long they'd have to last.

At precisely the appointed time, Treban arrived, looking like a clone of Naibu, except for minor differences. As he introduced us, Naibu noticed the scrutiny I was giving his former deputy.

'Are you surprised by the similarities, or the differences, Mark?'

'Both, I suppose.' I apologised. 'I mean the similarities are presumably a matter of convenience in construction. Sorry, that sounds rude, but you know what I mean …'

'I believe "No offence taken" is the right response, Mark. But the differences are rather more than simply allowing us to tell each other apart. We have other means for doing that. When we are initially activated, we look almost identical. But as we receive our programming, differences start to appear. I must admit, nobody really understands why. I have a theory it is because no two artificial brains are identical – they are too complex for that. So, as we receive input, which increasingly diverges as we become more specialised, this seems to be reflected in our appearance. It is subtle, but I like to think it gives us some personality. Were you ever to meet Admiral Zoltan, you would notice a marked difference immediately. It was not built into him on activation, it simply reflects who – or what – he has become.'

'I am pleased to meet you all,' said Treban, after first greeting his friend and colleague and the soldiers he had saved from termination. 'I understand what we are about to do and will play my part. We must move immediately, Naibu, there is only limited time before I am missed. We must complete our task quickly.'

Naibu nodded and turned to us.

'Evelyn, you and your team can only accompany us to the edge of the area in which the weapon is kept. We will start immediately.'

He led us through a series of passages delving more deeply into the android vessel. Given its size, I assumed we would have to travel for anything up to ten kilometres to reach our objective, but we were there in just one.

'Either the Decimator is larger than we'd guessed from Eddie's plan,' I opined, 'or we misunderstood.' I was careful to avoid the word "misled". Naibu was doing so much for us, there was no need to insult his integrity.

'Both are partly correct, Mark,' replied Naibu who, as we approached the end of our mission, had adopted more frequent use of our first names. 'The weapon is very large, but it is also eccentric, in terms of its location. It is to one side of the central engine and computer complex, on the opposite side to your initial incursion through the exhaust tube, which is why your team couldn't have succeeded anyway. The massive bulk of the Decimator would have protected much of the ship from an engine explosion. Only its own destruction can ensure the entire vessel is vaporised. We are here.'

We had come to a halt in front of the largest and heaviest door I'd ever seen. It was at least fifteen metres tall and twice as wide, apparently capable of being withdrawn into the wall on either side. Set into it was a smaller door, the size of a man. Or android. It was through this Naibu and Treban must pass.

'Beyond this door is a vacuum and intense radiation, as well as zero gravity,' he told Evelyn. 'You and your men must hold it with Sergeant Chukka, to protect us in case our presence is detected. It will take us thirty minutes to cross the radiation zone. Once beyond it we will be safe from attack and you can withdraw. We will allow you a further two hours to reach the Endeavour and make good your escape before we detonate the device. It will take half an hour to become critical and destroy the entire vessel, so you must be well away by then. From when we pass through this door, you will have three hours to make good your escape.'

I found myself unwilling to part from this remarkable ambassador for his people. To me, Naibu was a beacon of hope in an increasingly threatening Galaxy. Or at least the solar system, which was all I had travelled. Yet I could see the importance of what he was about to do and how its success was vital to humanity. If man was to survive, let alone expand throughout the cosmos, he must succeed. I wasn't alone in recognising his importance.

'Commander Naibu, there must be another way.' It was Treban who spoke for us all.

'You know there isn't, my friend,' replied the other. 'This ship has done too much damage and its leader will never alter his opinion about the need to destroy humanity. It – and he – must be removed. It is my responsibility. And only you and I can give the necessary command sequences. Even the sergeant cannot help in there.'

'Someone must take our message to the Supreme Council, Naibu,' said Treban. 'It should be you. It must be you. Who else can speak with the necessary authority?'

'And yet there is no alternative.'

'Yes, there is, commander.' Eddie had accompanied us for so long, his presence was easy to forget. Yet when he spoke, it was always to make a significant contribution. 'I can perform your function adequately. I was built to withstand high levels of radiation – and, like you, I do not require oxygen or gravity to operate. Give me the command sequences and I will replicate them faultlessly.'

I was horrified at the thought of losing Eddie; my only link to Earth. Yet on reflection, I wondered how much I really cared about my former home? My life seemed now to revolve around Evelyn and the Martians. They were my people as much as anyone, now my planet was devoid of human life. Albert would carry on working for a very long time, but unless I returned, he would have nobody to serve and would eventually cease to operate. Then Earth would be devoid of intelligence.

Unless I returned …

Evelyn looked a little red-eyed and I wondered whether this was sympathy for my impending loss – we all knew Eddie was right – or because she too would miss our companion. It was Treban who spoke.

'The robot is correct, Naibu. It and I will initiate the auto-destruct sequence and you must return with the Martians and find a way to communicate with the Supreme Council on Centauri; to convince them of the need for cooperation rather than conflict. This will be my legacy and I do not wish it to be wasted.'

There were no goodbyes. Naibu punched a complex command code into the control pad on Eddie's chest before nodding to Treban and opening the door through which the newly promoted commander and Eddie must pass, entering irrevocably into an airlock.

Once through the airlock, Treban noticed complete silence. He and the short robot were in a vacuum which prevented any sound from reaching their sensors. They now communicated only by radio link – and that in binary code. It was fast and allowed no room for misunderstandings.

'We have a long way to go in very little time,' Treban said. 'As gravity reduces, it will be more difficult to propel ourselves forward. Do you have internal thrusters?' Eddie indicated he had, although they were of limited power and duration. 'We will only need them one way. As soon as we can no longer walk, you must use them to push us both towards the control area. The radiation may affect my circuits towards the end. Officers are not made to withstand these conditions for long, only engineering workers.'

Few obstacles impeded their progress and, but Eddie soon became aware of his companion becoming sluggish and was obliged to take hold of the android and use his thrusters to maintain onwards momentum. There was no weight involved, only mass. Forward movement was easy, but each time they needed to turn a corner along their tortuous route – deliberately designed to prevent incursion – the robot had to expend more energy to move the mass than he'd allowed for.

'Have we much further to go, commander? I fear my power reserves might not suffice.' It was several moments before Treban replied. An eternity in computer terms.

'We are almost there … my friend. My functioning is impaired … I am preserving what energy I have for the command sequences we must enter. Just … a … few … minutes … more.'

Suddenly, and unexpectedly, gravity returned, causing Eddie to drop to the ground, letting Treban fall at his feet.

'I am sorry, commander. I was unaware the gravitational field was active here. I am also detecting falling radiation levels.'

'I was … unprepared for the … change, myself.' Treban's speech became slightly less impaired, although he could tell considerable damage had been done to his positronic brain. Not that it mattered, provided he could fulfil his task. 'I hope this does not indicate some other defence of which Naibu and I are unaware.' This seemed unlikely to him, given his seniority. But with Zoltan, one never knew.

Walking more slowly than before, watchful for traps, the android and robot approached the command post. It was a pair of matching computer consoles set four feet above the ground. A convenient height for androids. Less so for a short mobile computer.

Treban activated the first screen.

The face of Zoltan appeared. It spoke.

'Identify yourself.'

Chapter 32 – The final betrayal

Zoltan was gradually becoming aware of strange happenings on his vessel. He was generally a lazy leader, but even he wondered where his new commander had disappeared to and whether the anomalous readings on his control panel – one available only to himself – had any significance. His habitual reaction to anything unusual was to call for someone, formerly Naibu, latterly Treban. With neither available, he had no obvious individual to refer to. Then he had an idea.

'Chief Engineer Yargot, report to me immediately,' his sharp tone into the communicator leaving no room for doubt about his frustration. Delay would have consequences for everyone, not just those who had inconvenienced him. The engineer arrived faster than seemed possible. Zoltan wasted no time on pleasantries. 'What is the meaning of these data?'

Yargot looked at the screen in growing disbelief. Forgetting protocol, he leant right over the seated admiral and punched several sequences of numbers and figures into the keyboard, before standing back and to attention. This was likely to cost him his existence. Not because it was his fault, but because he'd become the bearer of bad news. Something nobody on the Zoltan-1 wanted to do.

'Sir. Someone has gained access to the Decimator. There are two signals coming from the control area. One is an android; the other is like nothing I have ever seen before.'

Zoltan's eyes flashed a dangerous red, reflecting overheating of the circuitry behind them – something which should never happen in an android.

'How did they get there?' The question was absurd, since the engineer couldn't possibly know. But Zoltan was beyond logic. Temporarily, Yargot hoped. 'Get some troops in there and destroy them before they can do any damage.' The volume of his voice increased uncharacteristically. 'DO IT NOW.'

✷

'They should have reached the control area by now,' Naibu said. 'We must be prepared for visitors. Spread out in defensive formation.' The soldiers, including Pakeman and Evelyn, knew precisely where to stand. For me it was a new experience, despite my simulator training. Evelyn said I should stand by her – probably for my own protection, rather than any combat value I might offer. She looked after me like a little sister.

Nine of us took positions to defend the door through which Treban and Eddie had passed half an hour earlier and waited. For some time, nothing happened.

'We've little more than two hours to get clear of the ship before the explosion,' I whispered to Evelyn. 'Shouldn't we be moving? It will take at least ninety minutes to get back to the Endeavour.'

Evelyn looked at Naibu for his agreement to our withdrawal. He looked worried.

'I cannot get any readings from Treban,' he said. 'If we move now, there is still a chance someone might get though and try to prevent them from activating the self-destruct commands. I must stay here and prevent anyone getting access for at least another hour and a half. The rest of you should leave immediately, or we all risk being destroyed.'

As he spoke the last word, a beam of light shot across the cavernous room in our direction. We'd been detected. Escape was now academic. All we could do was to prevent the failure of our mission by stopping the androids from reaching the Decimator's control area. Pakeman and the androids under Sergeant Chukka's command fired back without the need for orders. Everyone understood what was required of us. Evelyn and I opened fire, too. Me with less accuracy than anyone else, although even my contribution helped pin down the attackers, who had no idea how many intruders they were up against. We, on the other hand, knew there were fifty of them. At least this was the number Naibu – senior officers had special access to data of which their juniors were unaware – had been able to detect when the assault began. Within seconds there were only thirty-five, such was the intensity of our firepower. Thanks to our better positioning, we were largely protected from inwards fire. Even so, one by one, Chukka's men were picked off. Soon there were only six of us defending the door against five times as many androids.

'Identify yourself,' repeated Zoltan's image on the computer screen.

'Commander Treban,' signalled Eddie, 'he cannot see you, or he would know. Perhaps this is an automated system showing a representation of your leader. Let us input the initial codes and see what happens.'

'We cannot initiate the self-destruct sequence for at least two hours, or our friends will not have time to escape,' replied the android.

'Is there anything we can do to prevent incursion if our friends fail, commander?'

'No. At least, there are no additional defences of which I am aware.'

'What if we were able to intensify the radiation field? Would that be sufficient to disable even those androids built to withstand it?' The term "built", used between robot and android, couldn't appear pejorative; the humans had been careful to avoid it.

'Probably. Enough to prevent them reaching us, I believe. But even if we can, that will not help our friends to escape. If there is an attack, they will either be destroyed by the soldiers, or trapped and die in the explosion.' He paused. 'What have you in mind?'

Eddie had been studying the controls in front of him and analysing their capabilities. He was, after all a computer, rather than an artificially intelligent humanoid. His processing power was entirely dedicated to science, not sophisticated locomotion and other functions which androids emulated.

'We can cause a leak in the cooling system to increase the radiation in the passages through which we passed tenfold. It will not affect us here, so we can continue to wait for the time to detonate, without fear of interruption. I believe I can get a message to Naibu to this effect.'

'How? I have lost my internal communication with him.'

'By using the ship's systems.'

Eddie didn't wait for approval. He extended his lower supports, so he was level with the control panel and, ignoring the blank face of Zoltan, entered commands which would increase the pressure in the coolant pipes, causing a rupture within minutes. As soon as the fracture occurred, warning claxons sounded in the control compartment. Simply flicking a switch ensured the sound was replicated throughout the entire vessel. It would cause pandemonium amongst humans but, Eddie had calculated, in this instance the imperative for self-preservation would probably cause a similar impulse within the androids, at least initially.

As soon as the claxon sounded outside the confines of the weapon, the android force attacking us ceased firing; awaiting orders which didn't reach them in time. Knowing we had no alternative, we continued to fire and within seconds, we were alone.

'I don't know what Treban has done,' said Naibu, 'but I believe that is our signal to withdraw. There's something I must do first.' Without further comment, he walked over to a control panel and input a sequence of commands. If I didn't know better, I could have sworn he was smiling.

214

He finished quickly and gave the order to head back to the Endeavour.

'Won't we run into more troops, now they know we're here?' asked Evelyn.

'I think not, commander. I have just issued an order to abandon ship. Zoltan will try to countermand it, but he will not be able to do so. I have locked out his personal command protocol. He clearly omitted to cancel mine, so I accessed his. I don't suppose anyone will really leave, but there will be pandemonium as orders and counter-orders fly round at lightning speed. Let's go.' I noticed an unusual contraction in his speech. Was this exposure to us?

Moving quickly, we retraced our earlier steps, heading for the Endeavour. We reached the hangar, to find our shuttle apparently untouched. Perhaps nobody had noticed it – and once the alarm sounded, there'd been no time to question how we'd got here.

I looked at my watch as Pakeman closed the door and lifted off. It was two hours and twenty-nine minutes since Treban and Eddie had passed through the airlock. If they had achieved their objective, the self-destruct would already be in process and the Decimator starting to destroy itself. Soon, the engine room would explode – and the rest of the vessel follow. We'd accomplished our mission, but were about to lose some good friends in the process. And we still had to escape the effects of our handiwork, or the losses would include us.

We were slightly behind schedule, but I was confident Evelyn would be able to keep us safe.

Deep inside the Decimator, Treban and Eddie had little to do after initiating the sequence of commands which would turn the weapon in on itself and subsequently destroy the entire vessel. And anything within a radius of thousands of miles. Unlike humans, they felt no personal sense of regret, although Treban found himself hoping Naibu would be able to fulfil his self-imposed mission of initiating the process of peace with humanity. Eddie wondered whether Evelyn and his creator's protégé, as he had always viewed me, had escaped.

The end of the android vessel started with a deep rumble which could be felt as we left the hangar and flew into open space. It would be a close thing whether we escaped the billions of tons of destructive debris which would fly in all directions for as long as it took to strike an object sufficiently large to arrest its progress. If any fragment, however small, were to hit us we'd be instantly obliterated. As we sped away, Evelyn offered control of her craft to Naibu, confident he would be able to steer away from trouble more efficiently than her.

'No, commander,' he told her. 'This is your vessel, we will work together to avoid being struck by debris.'

That's how it should be from now on, I thought, as the two worked in harmony to keep us safe. We headed for the other side of Pluto, where the New Hope and Majestic awaited us.

Epilogue

As soon as we reached the New Hope, we were debriefed by Commander Adjara, accompanied by the other leaders in the same place as our previous meetings. The obvious sense of relief lighting their faces was tempered by a strange tightness round the eyes, the cause of which soon manifested itself.

'We know the mission was a success, and you are to be congratulated,' said Adjara as we sat round the conference table. 'There are, however a number of issues requiring clarification. Commander Naibu, are you aware of any messages being transmitted from the Centaurian vessel before its explosion? It seems unlikely it would fail to report events, yet we detected nothing.'

'As far as I can detect, commander, there were none. Admiral Zoltan was a proud officer, unlikely to admit failure. He would be more likely to have abandoned his command than admit to having lost it.'

'There is no evidence of any escape pods or vessels leaving the ship, Naibu,' said Major Xing. 'We monitored the area carefully, and continue to do so. I think we can assume your people have no idea what has happened. Even if a message could have been sent. It would surely take four years to reach Alpha Centauri.'

'Yes, major, but androids have a different perspective of time,' replied the commander. Four years would be the blink of an eye to them.

Xing made no response. Instead, it was Kerensa, the politician from Ganymede, who spoke.

'What will you do now, Commander?'

'I am determined to return to my home world and fight against the Supreme Council's apparent wish to destroy humanity. My men will accompany me. The journey will take a long time and during the intervening period, you need to be prepared for further attacks. You must continue to conceal your presence and improve your defences. There is no way you can assist in my efforts, because t ravelling vast distances in suspended animation would expose you to as much danger as the method you used to reach the stars previously.

If you could develop a faster means of transport it would be helpful, however. For humanity to survive – with or without we androids – you must be more proactive.'

'And what of you, Lieutenant Commander Starr, Mr Adams? Your homes are either abandoned or destroyed. Will you come and live with us on Ganymede? Or does the Last Hope offer greater appeal?' she asked, looking at each of us in turn. There was no doubt she would be involved in planning how to counter this threat, but didn't want to force our hands.

I was uncertain. Returning to Earth had little appeal, but what did I really want? My decision was made for me. Evelyn quietly took hold of my hand under the table and gave it a gentle squeeze of friendship. We must continue our partnership to counter the threat of which she first became aware, so long ago. I happily acquiesced to her unspoken invitation to work on with her.

'I think we'll return to Ganymede, for now.' She said simply, smiling and thinking of a certain leader there with whom she had a long-deferred date. 'There's important work to be done.'

<The end>

To leave a review, or for details of my other books, please visit: https://www.amazon.co.uk/Stephen-J.-Phillips/e/B07K4BWYZ1?

Printed in Great Britain
by Amazon

39768815R00126